Praise for *Barker House*

"HERE is a voice to listen to! Moloney's voice is as true as a voice can be. Concise, with the right details rendered perfectly, these sentences come to the reader with marvelous straightforwardness, clean as a bone. And they deliver." —Elizabeth Strout, Pulitzer Prize–winning author of *Olive Kitteridge* and *Olive, Again*

"Without romanticizing, demonizing, or candy-coating the work of his corrections officers, this novel-in-stories offers an experienced insider's view of their lives, in stainless-steely prose that easily matches the best of Raymond Carver and John Fante." —Tony Tulathimutte, Whiting Award–winning author of *Private Citizens*

"*Barker House* does not remotely read like a debut but more as the seasoned work of a writer with enormous gifts. With a keen eye for essential detail and a playwright's ear for dialogue, Moloney lays bare the inner workings of a county jail with a writerly passion utterly devoid of sentimentality or artifice of any kind. The result is a deeply satisfying work that will reach into the hearts and minds of many, many readers." —Andre Dubus III, author of *House of Sand and Fog*

"*Barker House* aims its razor-sharp gaze at the machinery of mass incarceration—and the men and women at its controls. Moloney's frank and humanizing depiction is lush with regret, longing, cruelty, and hope." —Robin Wasserman, author of *Girls on Fire*

"When it comes to the American penal system, David Moloney shows us that there are many insides. The interiors of the heart. The secret depths of the soul. The imprisoned, the imprisoners, their children, their spouses and partners, the strangers whose lives they've touched with violence, grace, or accident. They're all there inside the prison, and they're all here inside this book. Moloney is the best kind of writer, both powerful and graceful, and *Barker House* is an unforgettable book." —Wiley Cash, *New York Times* bestselling author of *The Last Ballad* and *A Land More Kind Than Home*

"Welcome to America, where the neglect of human beings has become a celebrated business model. **Barker House is a novel as important as Ted Conover's groundbreaking nonfiction *Newjack: Guarding Sing Sing* when it comes to this country's increasing inequities of class and mass incarceration.** Moloney is compassionate and authoritative and hugely moving in his portraits of those left behind by the heartless for-profit systems we set into motion and then ignore." —Jim Shepard, author of *The World to Come*

"**How fortunate we are that a brilliant and honest storyteller was embedded in the American prison system as a corrections officer for years.** Moloney went to the underworld and came back. The setting in *Barker House* has the unmistakable aspect of a real place, the dialogue the unmistakable ring of real speech. I loved my visits to this terrible kingdom." —**Benjamin Nugent, winner of the Paris Review's 2019 Terry Southern Prize**

"**A deeply felt novel about the soul-sucking grind of life at the margins of the labor force.** The men and women whose interwoven stories comprise this unforgettable debut aren't the prisoners, *they're the guards*, and yet their lives are hardly less violent, precarious, and desperate than the lives of the people under their authority." —**Justin Taylor, author of *Flings***

"A 'slaughterhouse,' writes David Moloney in his striking debut novel, *Barker House*, describing the decaying state of America's jails, the depths of that hell, and the lonely lot of jailers who are as trapped in their lives as the prisoners. **Moloney's spare prose and painful tales grab the reader by the throat and won't let go.**" —**Jean Trounstine, activist and author of *Boy With a Knife: A Story of Murder, Remorse, and a Prisoner's Fight for Justice***

BARKER HOUSE

BARKER HOUSE

DAVID MOLONEY

BLOOMSBURY PUBLISHING
NEW YORK · LONDON · OXFORD · NEW DELHI · SYDNEY

BLOOMSBURY PUBLISHING
Bloomsbury Publishing Inc.
1385 Broadway, New York, NY 10018, USA

BLOOMSBURY, BLOOMSBURY PUBLISHING, and the Diana logo are
trademarks of Bloomsbury Publishing Plc

First published in the United States 2020

The text on pages 18–31 was published in slightly different form as
"Bubble Time" in *Salamander* no. 49, Fall/Winter 2019–2020.

The text on pages 32–49 was adapted from "Dzole, Our Champion,"
Guernica, September 17, 2018.

The text on pages 101–24 was published in slightly different form as
"Property" in *Yale Review* 108, no. 1, March 2020.

This is a work of fiction. Names, characters, businesses, places, events,
locales, and incidents are either the products of the author's imagination
or used in a fictitious manner. Any resemblance to actual persons, living
or dead, or actual events is purely coincidental.

Bloomsbury Publishing Plc does not have any control over, or
responsibility for, any third-party websites referred to or in this book. All
internet addresses given in this book were correct at the time of going to
press. The author and publisher regret any inconvenience caused if
addresses have changed or sites have ceased to exist, but can accept no
responsibility for any such changes.

ISBN: HB: 978-1-63557-416-6; eBook: 978-1-63557-417-3

LIBRARY OF CONGRESS CATALOGING-IN-PUBLICATION DATA

Names: Moloney, David, 1984– author.
Title: Barker House / David Moloney.
Description: New York, NY: Bloomsbury Publishing, 2020.
Identifiers: LCCN 2019013382 | ISBN 9781635574166 (hardcover) | ISBN
9781635574173 (ebook)
Classification: LCC PS3613.O48 B37 2020 | DDC 813/.6—dc23
LC record available at https://lccn.loc.gov/2019013382

2 4 6 8 10 9 7 5 3 1

Typeset by Westchester Publishing Services
Printed and bound in the U.S.A. by Berryville Graphics Inc., Berryville,
Virginia

To find out more about our authors and books visit
www.bloomsbury.com and sign up for our newsletters.

Bloomsbury books may be purchased for business or promotional use.
For information on bulk purchases please contact Macmillan Corporate
and Premium Sales Department at
specialmarkets@macmillan.com.

For May and Cal

If you really want to know someone, work with them.

—DAD

Part I

KINGDOM

I work alone on the Restricted Unit in the Barker County Correctional Facility in New Hampshire. It's a semi-circular room, the curved wall lined with nine cells. Most of the day, the inmates press their faces to scuffed windows, silent. There are no bars. The architects went with rosewood steel doors. Rosewood: the color of merlot.

On Tuesday and Saturday mornings I supervise inmates while they shave in their cells. We don't leave them alone with razors. I try to talk with them, like we're just in a locker room, hanging out while one of us shaves. Some don't talk. I imagine that, cutting their whiskers before a scratched plastic mirror, they think of the other mirrors they've shaved in front of, the rooms those mirrors were in, and maybe that keeps them silent.

Tuesday. Inmate Bigsby is shaving. He's talkative. Not *crazy* crazy, but it's always tough to tell.

"This scar, right here," says Bigsby as a stroke down his cheek reveals a cambered wound, "was when I broke from the sheriffs." The single blade on Bigsby's flimsy disposable couldn't shave a teenage girl's happy trail but the inmates make do and pull at their skin.

There is a common perception—you see it in movies—that inmates don't want to talk about their crimes. But they do. They depend on their pasts, their scars, to prove they were something else. In what standing, that doesn't matter.

"I'm not familiar with the sheriff story." I press my fingertips together. My feet are in a boxer's stance. Even though Bigsby has never been violent in Barker House, that could change. Shaving cream drips into his mouth and he spits into the metal sink. Behind him are a single metal bed, a tiny window above it, and a yellow glow-light dimmed by heavy Plexiglas.

"It was on all the news," Bigsby says with a smile. His rough voice sounds practiced. He's been on RU for two months. His arms are tattooed in old-school ink, the black turned green and smeared. He's lived in halfway houses, shelters, jails, prisons. He says he's even squatted in people's basements for weeks at a time, the homeowners never the wiser.

One cell over, Inmate Sanchez punches the wall. The meat of his fat hand smacks with each blow. He groans, slows, stops, begins again. Bigsby looks over his shoulder as if to see through the wall, as if his concern could stop the dim-witted Hispanic man from harming himself. He shakes his head.

"His extension was denied," Bigsby explains. "Trial starts Monday."

I lean outside the cell's threshold with my eyes still on Bigsby and tell Sanchez to cut the shit. He doesn't. To pass the time, I ask Bigsby to tell me his story.

"It was back when I was facing weapons charges. I was a 'three strikes' guy with none left to give." He runs the blade over the curve of his ear. "Leaving court, they got two old-timer sheriffs on me. Guys could barely put the leg shackles on. I kicked one over and ran, more like skipped. And when I saw the Nashua, I jumped in."

"That's hardcore."

"I floated for a while. It was quiet and I tried not to move much," he says. "I thought I got away. Then I heard the dogs barking. Those fuckers can swim."

The punching continues.

"You want to go in the Chair again, Sanchez?" He's been in it once after he tried to drown himself in his toilet. He keeps punching.

Bigsby stops shaving. "You can't leave me with half a face of hair," he says to me. "Sanchez, chill, amigo."

I wave my hand at Bigsby out of view of Sanchez: *I'm not serious.* Bigsby continues his shave. I am serious, though. If Sanchez breaks his hand it'll be my ass in a cast. The punches come slower but harder. Bigsby's mirror wiggles. He stops shaving and taps the head of the razor on the sink, half his face still slathered in shaving cream.

"Imagine he knocked his girl around like that."

I put my hand out. "Give me the razor," I say. "I got to deal with this asshole."

Bigsby pauses. "I'm not done, CO. I look like a sideshow freak." He looks afraid because he knows the outcome here. Half-shaven until Saturday. A hard punch hits the wall and Bigsby flinches. I motion again and he hands me the razor. I pull his cell door shut and lock it; he shouts through the clear window how fucked up it is to leave him like that. Bigsby thinks we're boys because I let him talk and sometimes I talk back. But now I'm just another asshole cop, he says. He kicks his door and Sanchez decides to take a break from punching his wall to punch his door, which makes more noise. If they were bars, I wonder if the two men would take to striking them, if they would strike any partition.

I radio my sergeant. Over the open airwaves, I'm sure he and every other screw with a two-way can hear, in between the bangings of fists on metal doors, pleas for me to go fuck myself.

———————

I DRIVE THROUGH a light dusting of snow with the radio off, focused on the rhythmic screech of the windshield wipers. The roads are guarded by curved snowbanks, their whiteness soiled by blown exhausts and salt and sand. Even though my DUI charges were dropped because the Statey misplaced my Breathalyzer sample, my captain still required me to attend counseling. I was reluctant. I'd gotten the drinking under control on my own.

I meet Jerry on Wednesday afternoons in Nashua. It turned out to be sort of interesting, therapy. I like to pre-game what I'm going to say to Jerry, to keep him on task. He's a rambler. He gets paid by the hour. His practice shares a duplex with a children's dentist. Sometimes kids and their parents pass me on the stairs, the kids' eyes puffy, holding bags with toothbrush heads sticking out the tops, rewards for sitting still in the chair. When I knock on Jerry's door, I can hear the sounds of the waiting room on the floor above: toys being pounded against the carpet, and the woodwinds of cartoons.

This is my third Wednesday. Last week, for homework, Jerry asked me to watch some bullshit Sandra Bullock movie about rehab. I didn't. He won't follow up.

Jerry starts off on his favorite subject: the injustices perpetrated in my place of employment. The House is for-profit, so we spend as little money as possible on the food, and we share a doctor with two other counties. He talks about that, instead of my drinking, or my arrest.

I don't bite. He sighs and hoists his sneaker up onto his thigh. He's big and fat and his black shirt is half-tucked into jeans. His clerical collar is cockeyed. As a certified counselor, he says, he's offended by the abuse and neglect of prisoners as a business model.

"I used to be a counselor," I say.

This works. "Drugs?" He wiggles in his chair, interest piqued.

"Kids. At the old mental hospital in Raymond," I say and Jerry lets his leg fall back to the floor. "I left two years ago."

"People say terrible things about that place," he says like I don't know. "June. You remember, my daughter." He turns the picture frame on his desk toward me. "She's going to BU for psychology. She wants to help kids, too."

"I mainly wrestled with them on dirty rugs," I say, "during restraints. I'd do eight to ten restraints a shift, sometimes more. To help them."

"June is tender," he says and turns the picture back out of my sight. "I see her being more on the clinical side."

"We hated the clinicians. The kids did, too."

Jerry nods. "When she was ten, she helped a boy home after a bicycle wreck. The kid hit a tree, got all cut up," he tells me. "I picture her doing things along those lines."

"These kids don't have bike accidents. They hurt themselves on purpose."

Jerry takes a butterscotch from a jar on his desk, unwraps it, puts it in his mouth.

"And if we hurt them or got rough," I say, "that meant we cared."

Jerry puts a finger under his nose and slurps at the hard candy. Behind his cluttered desk, which is covered in newspaper and Styrofoam coffee cups, a clock on the wall ticks through the silence. The room is just a tad bigger than an inmate's cell. All I can smell is butterscotch and coffee.

He probably expected this to be another sixty minutes of story time, two Irish guys talking about drinking, fighting, love. He told me on our first week he quit drinking twenty-two years ago. He said cops back then didn't give DUIs. They'd throw your keys in the snow and give you a ride home. He wished they'd given him one, saved him decades.

"You got rough with the kids?" he finally asks.

Our time is almost up. I want to tell Jerry about José but there isn't time. I wouldn't be able to explain him: a twelve-year-old son of a prostitute, a boy who liked starting fires, hurting dogs, playing with Legos. He wore a fanny pack he found in the trash and hid marbles, bouncy balls, broken Nintendo DS games in it. He cursed like a john. He was wiry and strong, which turned out to be a problem.

The night he died, José chose to wait until lights-out to ask to do his laundry. He'd get stuck on a task and, until it was completed, would struggle for days before he could move on. Christine didn't want to press the issue and walked José to the laundry room down the hall. Only a minute later, she yelled for staff, and I left my post outside the boys' bedrooms and ran to find José grappling with her. Christine was petite but strong, bragged about her CrossFit PRs.

I secured one of José's wrists and twisted it clockwise until he was rendered facedown on the floor. Christine got hold of his other wrist. As we were trained, the two of us proned José out. He feigned defeat—he always did—then attempted to free himself. Christine and I shifted into the next stage of the restraint and sat against José's armpits, pressed our backs against one another's. We pulled his arms taut against our abdomens. It was methodical, practiced, by the book. But José wouldn't concede. And then Christine told me he wasn't struggling on her end and asked me if he was struggling on mine.

I turn to the photo of June. "She's pretty," I say. "The kids liked the pretty clinicians."

I WATCH TV. Infomercials are the only things worth watching. Power washers. Root shovels. An indoor-garden kit. No one wants to hear it. There's Jerry, but he's too responsive. I don't call my parents. My friends are gone. If Christine and I had anything it was dissolved that night in October at ten minutes to eleven. My father took José's death well. He brags about my new pension. I can't tell him about the heaviness that crawls up my chest when I sleep. It'll disturb his current positive opinion of me. My mother took José's death well. She went to all the services, cut out his obituary from the newspaper. She looks at me like I worked at an abortion clinic.

On the back of a magazine on my coffee table, the ad on the page for a spray deodorant has a good deal of white space. I've filled it with the names of products and the phone numbers you call to order them. Showtime Rotisserie. Snuggie. Acne something? I don't have acne and must've been buzzed when I watched that infomercial.

A man cuts through a soda can with a knife. He also promises a fifty-year warranty. Fighting the urge to make a purchase, I down another Luksusowa and orange soda water and get out of the apartment.

I pull into the gravel parking lot, the tires crunching frozen snow. I stand outside my car and stare into the cold night sky, try to get my head right. The Blue Moon is the size of a diner.

Surrounded by dense wetlands, without neon or a flashy exterior, it can pass for one.

I don't make eye contact with the bald bouncer. He looks like an ex-inmate and I don't want to get into that kind of conversation. He checks my ID and doesn't ask any questions. I skip getting a drink and head toward the solo dance area behind a maroon curtain. For twenty dollars, you get a private dance in a stall, its door similar to a bathroom stall's. There are lines of stalls with other men and slightly attractive women inside of them. I find Michelle. She told me once her brother is autistic. She doesn't mind my stories. Even though she encourages me, I don't touch her.

"You don't seem like the type of woman that enjoys wearing bras," I say. Michelle has decent-sized breasts and they look real, having a slight swing to them as she moves. Her brown skin is clear of blemishes. Her breath smells like Fireball.

"No," she says, "too uncomfortable. I like being free."

"You might enjoy the AHH Bra," I say. "No hooks or wires."

"Never heard of it." She sits on my lap. "I don't excite you?"

"You do," I say. "I wrote down the number, in case you're interested."

She stands and puts her hands on my cheeks. "I bet you have a great smile."

"Don't tease me."

"I want to see it," she says. "Good! I made Tommy smile."

BIGSBY HAD AN active night. He was able to get a few other inmates to rock the unit. They rolled up spitballs, slid them out through the four-inch space under their doors. The dayroom floor was covered with them when I arrived for my shift. The officer I relieved, Josephs, was sitting in the middle of them, reading a fat paperback with his flashlight. He likes to call the unit "a well-oiled machine."

"He's hot about his face," says Josephs, of Bigsby. "I called him Two-Face *once* and he ruined my shift." He indicates the spitballs.

Josephs leaves the unit. I don't make any unexpected moves, at first—just gather up the spitballs in my palm, brush them off my gloved hands into the trash. No one says anything; I hear the occasional giggle. When it's time for showers, I begin with Sanchez, as usual, and wait until he is comfortable under his cone of steam and hot water, face downturned. Then I unlock the recreation yard door and kick it open. It's January. The icy breeze cuts through my uniform.

There's cursing and shouting. But Sanchez showers nonetheless. When he's done, I hand him a towel, and he brings it to his face, but then it falls, his kinked fingers incapable of gripping it. The towel sits in a puddle on the concrete shower floor, with the cold wind blowing over it. Sanchez's curly hair drips water over his eyes, and his pubic hair is thick and hides almost all of his penis.

"That's the only one you get today," I tell Sanchez.

He shakes off like a dog and droplets hit my face. I flinch. I can hear Bigsby laughing behind his cell door.

Sanchez picks up the sopping towel and rubs it on himself. His pink, peeling knuckles show fresh blood. It's eight o'clock. Outside the walls, the clanging doors, high above the snores and farts and stink of unflushed toilets and body odor, the sky unloads fluffy snow on the roads.

I tell Sanchez to cut the shit and go back into his cell. His hour of tier time isn't up yet, but the way his large body mopes around, his numb eyes following me, makes me want to cut his time short. Most inmates would complain about losing tier time but Sanchez never does. I've asked myself if he is playing a game, like some inmates do when they plan to plead insanity. But the state of his hands tells me he's not playing.

He walks naked into his cell and I key his door locked. He stands at the door, and I know how piercing the frigid water on his skin is. But he doesn't let me know he feels it.

Bigsby comes out next. He struts past me to the showers, his face divided, one side smooth, the other furry with gray hair. He stares at the open rec yard door. He grunts and goes behind the beige half-wall, me on the other side. I slam my boot on the stool of a dayroom table, my tan uniform tight, head freshly shaven, and I imagine he sees me as a person with power. He finishes undressing. His skin is white and seems to tighten from the cold.

"That's a real prick move to open the door like that," he says. "That's some old-school bullshit. I figured you better than that."

The door behind me leads to a small bricked-in rec yard with a basketball hoop with no net. We don't have a basketball to offer the inmates. There's nothing to do out there but walk around in circles. The walls are high and topped with chicken wire. Some snow has fought through and coated the ground.

"I wouldn't have put up with this shit before," Bigsby says and turns the shower on. He gets under the water and lets it run over his face. His fills his mouth with water and spits it high into the air. Steam runs out from over the half-wall and rises toward the ceiling lights, giving them the look of streetlights in fog.

———————

WHEN JOSÉ FIRST came into the hospital, he had nothing. "Indigent" is what we'd call an inmate like that. José had nothing because it'd burnt in a fire. His mother left him alone. He couldn't find his dog. José lit a candle and slid it under the bed for light. The dog came out from under the bed, and I imagine they played, rolled around like kids do with their pets, the dog licking José's earlobe. The bed burnt first. Then, three units in the jam-packed downtown apartment building. The only living thing not to make it off the top floor was the dog.

I went through my closet and drawers and filled a trash bag. Old baseball jerseys, Patriots garb, T-shirts I'd cut the sleeves off of. The only rule of the ward when donating was it had to be anonymous. Only organic relationships. The kids came from places where possessions meant everything, especially because of who they came from. I remember watching José drive toy cars across the carpet, making beeps and vrooms. He was wearing the green Parks and Recreation T-shirt I wore when I worked for the department in high school. I wanted to tell him about that job, how I taught kids to swim. To jump rope, flirt with girls. I knew he wouldn't have listened to anything I had to say unless I started by telling him he was wearing my shirt.

———————

THE MUSTER ROOM is full of officers chatting about new restaurants and superhero movies, hangovers, who was at the bar last and didn't make it to work. Six ten-foot tables face the front of the room. Four sergeants are lined up behind the lectern at the helm. The brick walls are bright yellow and littered with inspirational posters. At 211 degrees, water is hot. At 212, it boils. With boiling comes steam. And steam can power a locomotive.

Lt. Hobson reads off the roster, plugs me into RU, then goes over the notes from the previous two shifts. He says Bigsby spent the night throwing fecal matter out of his cell. He refused to stop when directed. Bigsby claimed he wasn't being treated right, that the jail was screwing with him. Hobson cautions us against walking by Bigsby's cell. When he's done reading off the notes, he dismisses the room but tells me to stay back. The muster room begins to clear. Hobson has a blond crew cut, a filled-out chest and shoulders, and reflective insignias in two long rows pinned over his heart. He stays quiet and inattentive until we are the only two left.

"Bigsby," he says as he looks at me. "I personally supervised his shave this morning. He claims you left the rec door open during his shower. Cut off his shave halfway through. Don't give him a platform."

I nod. Hobson obviously forgets Sanchez's incident during shaves.

"Stop fucking with the rec door," says Hobson. He squeezes my shoulder as he passes me out of the muster room. "Oh," he says. He turns around, his hand on the doorframe. "Bigsby told me to tell you he's waiting for you."

Sweaty Officer Josephs is wearing purple nitrile gloves, and he's tying a red hazardous waste bag, which surely contains Bigsby's shit, by the inner door to the unit. But there's no smell of shit, no trace of it. Josephs watches me in the full-dome mirror mounted in the center of the unit. I watch him as he watches me while I write my opening log. It's clear from his silence that he blames me for his bad night. He tosses the bag near the trash barrel and walks behind me, grabs his log and slides it to me. I sign him off. Once he's gone I look for Bigsby in the grate of his door, but his face doesn't come.

I'm anxious to make my rounds. Whatever I do, I don't want to cede power to Bigsby. The eight bodies on my unit are asleep.

I key open Sanchez's cell for tier time at 0725 hours, kick the bottom side of his metal bed with my boot, and he startles awake. He's nude. His room smells like wet dog hair. He sits up and walks out of the cell and straight into the showers. He turns a shower on and I open the rec yard door and let the wintry air pour in.

Bigsby, awake, immediately comes to his window and starts punching and kicking the cell door. Freshly shaven, his face again symmetrical. We look at each other from ten feet away.

Bigsby's banging awakens other inmates. Silently, their faces surface behind their windows.

Sanchez turns off the shower and shivers. I bring him his towel from the half-wall. Bigsby is still kicking. The other inmates watch and allow Bigsby to have the floor. I hand the towel to Sanchez and he drops it, his fingers crippled, unable to grasp even air. In the full-dome mirror, I see Bigsby's arm creep out from under his door and throw a handful of shit into the dayroom. I don't turn or look back. He's yelling, "Shut the door! Shut the door!" like a protester. I've never heard him sound so alive.

Sanchez stands over his towel, shaking uncontrollably, wild, making faces that remind me of a fish in a net. He starts to cry. I pick up the towel and begin with his shoulder. I dry down his arm and he holds it out as if we've done this before. He cries as I dry his chest, his legs. He lets me dry his injured fingers, and then his entire body.

T oday his world was not serene, because just before lunch, Menser lost his cuff key.

A pleasing day for Scott O'Brien would be working on Max with enough Bubble time to end each shift, driving straight to the gym while sipping iced black coffee mixed with chocolate whey protein powder. After that, he'd drink. O'Brien wanted to do all these things alone. He had no problem with running tier time alone, then enjoying the quiet control room on Max, the Bubble. Where boots could be put up, eyes shut behind blackout shades, and there were no cameras.

He'd let inmates out of their cells in groups of four; a three-to-one inmate-to-officer ratio was the policy on Max. The extra inmate per group would shave two hours off his shift expectation, allowing him to nap after lunch. The risk was worth it; rarely did the inmates act out on his shift. He found he could get more done without his partner, Menser. In his overstuffed uniform, Officer Eric Menser was a cumbersome load. He'd mishear names and take out the wrong personal property boxes before tier time. He would nod when O'Brien gave him instructions but then go and do something else, like wipe down dayroom tables or fart into the cracks of inmates' doors and laugh. "The spray bottles, Menser. Have the inmates clean their cells," O'Brien would remind him. Without Menser, O'Brien could do these simple tasks by himself, which saved the stress of micromanaging an officer who'd been on the unit since before O'Brien graduated high school.

O'Brien also enjoyed the relative silence of hearing nothing more than showers running, inmates pleading with baby mamas on the unit phone, and toilets flushing. During routine tier time, O'Brien would watch the clock and prep the next group of inmates to get a head start. Any time, minutes even, he'd take advantage of before lunch. It only made the rest of the shift work in his favor. O'Brien wasn't obsessive-compulsive; rather, he was strategic in pursuing the things that eased his mind, which were Bubble time, gym, drinking, in that order. His last girlfriend had left him two years ago after he proved to be noncommittal, blowing off a trip to San Diego for her sister's wedding. He couldn't afford the vacation time, which he saved for a golf trip that year in Ireland. He never went on the trip, and he settled into this routine. Whenever things got to a certain point with a woman, he'd say to curious friends, "We aren't really a thing."

The day began with Menser choosing to start out on the floor with O'Brien, which put Greenly in the Bubble. O'Brien had been working with Menser for over three years and found ways of delegating chores to him to get him out of the way. He'd watch Menser sweep the already clean top tier, in oblivious fulfillment, and feel slightly bad for the guy, like he'd thrown an invisible ball to a dog. If Menser seemed ambitious, O'Brien would then give him a real chore, and later regret it. The saddest part was watching Menser's decline in real time, not like some cheesy movie drama montage of despair. His depression became evident quickly: the sudden weight gain, heavy soda drinking, sick-time usage. He would say things like, "One day they'll shut this place down. Make us all grocery baggers."

That day, Menser seemed uncharacteristically excited. While Menser made the first round, O'Brien heard him greeting the inmates at their doors, and he took the lead in drawing out the tier time for the day and getting the right cells cleaned. Instead of feeling good for Menser, O'Brien was knocked off his rhythm and wished Menser had come in sullen, prepared to wipe cell door windows. He decided to keep out of Menser's way and let him tire himself out. They ran tier time efficiently, and the day was playing out to end with Menser and O'Brien sharing the Bubble, which still beat staying on the floor for the entire shift with the inmates.

Then Menser told O'Brien they had a problem. Menser didn't know where he lost his cuff key, or if he had brought it to begin with. O'Brien would normally retrace his steps, but in jail, and with Menser not remembering when or if he had it, the steps had variables. Any of the nine inmates on tier time could have swiped it. They would pat inmates down at the end of tier time, but there were blind spots on the human body. And if he lost it on a round, it would have fallen close enough to the cell doors where an inmate could have reached out from under his door and grabbed it.

Protocol, for any other unit besides Max, was to call the floor sergeant and inform him of the missing equipment. But there was a standing order for Max: any shit that happens down there goes straight to the lieutenant. Lt. Hobson had a strange affinity for Max because he had helped Operations draft the new security policies after the riots in 1999. It was still his house and little mistakes rode right up his ass. So of course O'Brien would prefer to find the cuff key himself. The problem was the cameras. They'd record the unit officers running around the unit looking for something they'd claim wasn't missing until Hobson was called. And Hobson would most certainly check the tapes.

O'Brien gave himself and Menser five minutes to sweep the dayroom, the showers, and the two closets to find it. Five minutes. Officer Greenly searched the Bubble.

"I honestly don't think I clipped it on this morning," Menser said. "I can picture it on my dresser."

Any other officer and maybe O'Brien would let it ride, would wait to find out from Menser later if he had in fact left it on his dresser. O'Brien had even lost one himself during his rookie year, and for that reason he kept four identical keys hidden in his locker. But he couldn't offer one of his replacement keys to Menser. He knew him well enough to work with him, but he couldn't involve him in a scheme so involved as covering up a missing key. He didn't trust Menser's wits. When he told Menser he was calling Hobson down, Menser shook his large domical head bizarrely, and it wobbled as if it had become unbound.

"I didn't have it," he said. "I shouldn't even have told you. Fucking snitch."

Menser's face was red, not embarrassed-red, more splotchy high-blood-pressure-red. He wouldn't look at O'Brien. He rubbed his neck with both hands, which seemed to bolt it back on. He collected himself, drank his Mountain Dew, and stood off behind a large blue pole in the center of the dayroom.

It reminded O'Brien of something his mother once said. He'd told her there was a boy in his class, much larger than all the other kids, who cried all the time, sat out of dodgeball, wept on the bleachers. O'Brien's mother, a middle school teacher, told him some kids had sensitive minds in big bodies. "It's like giving a baby a lighter, Scott. Dangerous, but it'll never figure out how to use it." O'Brien called Lt. Hobson over the radio.

Hobson was the kind of lieutenant who projected his feelings onto his subordinates. He was from Nebraska, waylaid by bad knees from a failed football career that brought him north. Hobson was in his forties, had thick traps, shoulders like he still had pads on; his white shirt tight around his chest and shoulders but loose on his midsection. He had a linebacker's body and a blond crew cut like a Marine, but O'Brien heard he had tried out for the Jaguars as a fullback, and as much as he came off as ex-military, it was all an act. When he read muster notes before shift, he had trouble reading, would sometimes stutter, then stop and apply a shitload of ChapStick, then pick up his place. Once, at lunch, O'Brien watched Hobson with disgust as he ate liver. He just stuck his fork in the gray organ and chewed off a big piece. Officer Markowski told Hobson it was gross, didn't he know what function the liver played in the body? And Hobson said, "To eat your own." They all laughed and Markowski was dumb enough to correct him. Hobson, with a piece of liver in his teeth, said, "That's how we say it from where I'm from."

Hobson pulled Menser into the sally port, a darkened passage, the only entrance and exit from the highly secured unit, and let into him. The heavy door prevented O'Brien from perfectly hearing the muffled ass-chewing coming from behind it. He wanted to hear how badly Menser was being berated.

O'Brien and Menser, supervised by Hobson, began the process of searching the inmates and their cells. O'Brien took the lead, tapped on the door grate, ordered the lone inmate inside to walk to the front of the cell, kneel facing the wall opposite the stainless steel toilet with his hands behind his back, fingers interlocked. Don't move. O'Brien waved his hand over his head, and Greenly flipped the panel switch from inside the Bubble, then the door slowly opened along a motorized belt. Once the door clanged open, O'Brien and Menser entered the cell, stood the inmate up by his biceps, and extracted him. Hobson patted the inmate down while O'Brien and Menser searched the inside. They would need to do this for all twenty-two isolation cells on Max.

None of the industrial green plastic mattresses O'Brien patted with his gloved hands, air vents he beamed a flashlight into, or light coverings he unscrewed and took down yielded anything. All that he found underneath the steel bedsteads were dried crusts from bologna sandwiches or apple cores covered in brown ants. It wore on O'Brien; conducting unclothed searches after clearing each cell; visually checking mouths, nostrils, armpits, fat rolls; ordering the inmates to lift their balls, in the midst of their own understandable aggravation, turn, bend and spread their cheeks; peering into unclean assholes, already knowing he wouldn't find the key. He could hear Hobson sighing heavily behind him. Each time O'Brien handed a piece of clothing to Menser, he was handing Menser empty, dispirited waistbands.

O'Brien knew that the remainder of his day was messed up. Bubble time was gone. They'd have to stay late writing reports. He wouldn't have time to hit the gym and drink.

O'Brien lifted weights. He wasn't huge; he came in at 170 pounds on most days (he weighed himself at the same time, nude, every morning). He believed in building dense muscle. So he lifted heavy weight, quickly, with no rest, like a cardio and strength workout-in-one, because he never wanted to go back to the fatness and double chin that caused him to fail his first physical fitness exam at the jail academy. And he was competitive. He wanted to become a white shirt, a sergeant, then lieutenant, and maybe captain one day. O'Brien was a keen observer of the obvious, and it was obvious that fat officers didn't get promotions. Captain Dixon was fit and seemed to take pride in standing alongside other fit and presentable white shirts at funerals, parades, and fallen officer 5Ks. Hobson usually ran in front of the House's crew, jogging in formation, chanting cadence led by Dixon, with Hobson holding their banner high above his head. Once, Officer Tully pulled out of the Race for Healing 5K halfway through. He claimed he had asthma but O'Brien, as he watched from the back of the pack while controlling his breathing, knew Tully's career had just hit the ceiling.

Another asshole and no key. The shift was coming to a close, and O'Brien knew he wouldn't get a workout in. And that would change the way he ate throughout the day. He was on strict calorie control. If he didn't exercise, he could take in exactly 2100 calories. On days he did work out, he could take in 2600 calories.

After backing out of cell 2089, which smelled like a former inmate, a rather savage man who reeked of shit and peanut butter, Hobson puffed his chest and O'Brien wondered if he'd ever work with Menser again on Max. He couldn't decide whether he was sad or relieved, like when a grandparent died. He concluded he would probably forgo the gym for drinking that night.

His drinking ritual disrupted his efficient, quiet workdays and also his ability to stay lean, among other things. And it might've been less a ritual than a habit, because he was conscious of it. Rituals were illogical, and drinking was not. He drank for the enjoyable process of drinking, and the end game (drunkenness) was hard to predict, but the journey was worth taking. His favorite drink was his third drink. The first was boarding the boat, the second was unknotting the mooring rope, and the third kicked the boat away from the dock.

After much trial and error with vodka tonics, red wine, and malt liquor, he settled on beer. Liquor and wine made him black out too quickly, missing that all-important state between buzzed and drunk. It was the hardest state to get to and appreciate. Anyone could sip three drinks then quit or get foolishly ambitious and shotgun twelve. It was the place right before drunk and far enough away from buzzed where he was most pleased with himself. So he drank light beer, which was easy to log into his calorie-counting app. Through research he uncovered that he wasn't alone in his quest, with the many websites dedicated to this endeavor, and he narrowed his choices of highest alcohol by volume to calories per serving to two beers: Natural Light and Michelob Ultra. With these two beers, preferably Natural Light because it was cheaper, he could fully control each stage, the pacing, and the calories. He knew he couldn't start before six P.M.; because his average pace was three beers an hour, he'd have to call it a night around ten, and that felt too early for him.

But Menser losing the cuff key, which in turn would make him miss the gym, meant five fewer drinks, unless he skipped his dinner of baked, skinless chicken on dry brown rice, meaning an even earlier end time. And pushing back the start time left idle time in between work and drinking. He could then maybe squeeze in the gym, bringing his calories back up, pushing back his bedtime, but losing his Bubble time already threw everything off and his coffee-protein drink that late in the day would really keep him up, so maybe the idea of pursuing the mind-easing ritual was misguided.

They didn't find the cuff key. Menser got a write-up. Hobson slammed the write-up on the muster room desk in front of Menser while he and O'Brien were writing informational reports for the lost equipment. Menser slid it under the report he was writing and didn't read it, forcing Hobson to leave the muster room without the satisfaction of seeing Menser's devastation. O'Brien sat close to him at the table and watched his face as he wrote. His reddish-blond eyebrows were hard to see. He had a redhead's paleness, freckles, light arm hair and facial hair, but he didn't have red hair. He wrote rapidly, his large fingers wrapped around the pen, the fresh sweat on his neck embellishing the salty white dried sweat on his collar, unwashed from previous days.

Some part of O'Brien wanted to invite Menser to his apartment, share the drinking process with him. But Menser seemed sad, and not the basic kind of sad. He wouldn't be able to get a few drinks in Menser and make fun of how Hobson can't read to cheer him up. To O'Brien, Menser was uncomfortably lost; his energy could take down everyone around him.

The locker room was empty. It was an hour into second shift and all the first shifters had cleared out. Menser changed into a T-shirt and sweatpants. He pulled the strings tight around his waist and tied a knot.

"Hitting the gym?" O'Brien asked.

"I'd like to," said Menser as he bent over on the bench and tied his shoes. "Solid chance I don't make it."

O'Brien turned to his open locker and hung up his uniform. He looked at the box of pens where he hid his cuff keys. It'd be simple. Hand one to Menser, send him to Hobson, they'd both say they found it in the locker room.

"Come over to my place later, have a drink."

Menser stood and slung his gym bag over his shoulder. "I don't drink," he said.

"Maybe they won't take you off Max," O'Brien said. "Guys have done worse."

They rode the elevator in silence. Menser had tucked his lips, kept an expression of determined eyes and embarrassed mouth, throughout the shift. O'Brien patted Menser on the shoulder when they got off the elevator.

"Don't sweat it, big guy," he said. "It's probably on your dresser."

Menser nodded and walked ahead of him without looking back. He walked through the parking lot and got into his truck, then drove off.

———————————

UNDER THE BRONZED four-light ceiling fan with two working bulbs, as it emitted a tender breeze on the lowest setting, the neighbors arguing over late-night Chinese food, O'Brien stared at his sweaty Natural Light and thought about Menser. He sat at the kitchen table in his apartment and behind him crackled free-range, antibiotic-free chicken nuggets in the toaster oven.

As meticulous as he was, there were times when he overshot the sweet spot of drunkenness and ended up eating calories he wouldn't dare log into his calorie app.

Those nights were rare, as he was usually able to feel the drunkenness coming when he had difficulty making out an electronic screen clearly with both eyes open (if he closed one eye and the visuals aligned, he knew he'd gone too far). If not that, it was his YouTube video selections (watching prairie dogs explode by .50 cal sniper fire). He left his phone right side up, unusually; he hoped to see Menser's text telling him the key was in fact on his dresser. And each beer he drank where the text didn't come, he moved to the fridge for another.

He ate the chicken nuggets, because he was hungry, but also because he wanted to sober up. When he got like this his self-destructiveness deepened. He'd wanted to put himself into a state where he could truly understand how Menser felt, like a medium channeling his pain, not with candles and incense or a deck of Death cards, but with Natural Lights. This attempt, of course, didn't work, and he only drank himself onto the cusp of forgetting. He chewed and swallowed, washed each bite down with beer. He had two beers left, maybe three.

After eating, he opened Paintbrush on his laptop, a program he'd never used before, and with one eye closed he began to draw Menser. Though crude with choppy lines, the final product did look like the guy. It was a profile view, his nose dipped down past his upper lip; his lips were big and bulging like he'd puckered them. O'Brien gave only one shot at the outline of his head and face. He put red dotted pimples on

Menser's neck but they looked like gunshot wounds. He erased them. He drew Menser in uniform, his stomach round, sagging over the pants. The profile view didn't do Menser's portrait any favors. O'Brien added a nice detail, he thought, the Barker County seal, on Menser's right shoulder, a pine tree inside a triangle with the year 1767. The numbers looked like a sloppy lowercase *m*. Sipping his beer between line strokes, he drew a large lighter next to Menser. Not a fashionable Zippo. Nothing fancy. Just an oversized lighter, too big to hold in his hand. It looked more like a candle.

Reviewing the drawing gave O'Brien a sense of desperation. He should've bailed him out. With one eye closed, he texted Menser, *I can rescue you*. Then, after another beer, *Right or wrong everyone deserves it*. And another beer, possibly emptying the fridge, waiting for Menser to text back, *Cannot forget what you're made from*.

Finally, Menser answered, *What are you talking about?*

You can redeem yourself. Faith in you buddy.

Whatever.

O'Brien felt better having reached out to Menser. At least the guy knew O'Brien wasn't intentionally out to get him. Hell, he didn't lose Menser's cuff key. He looked at the drawing again and decided to text it to Menser. With his phone, he lined up a picture and snapped it. O'Brien couldn't tell if he was too drunk or the picture quality was too poor. His one-eye trick wasn't lining the image up. He sent it anyway, then finished the last half of what he figured to be his last beer. He went down the hallway barefoot to the bathroom. While he pissed, he laughed. Menser would get a kick out of the drawing.

He went back to the table and with his finger, dabbed at the chicken nugget breadcrumbs, then licked them off. Menser texted him back.

Is that a computer screen? It's all wavy and fucked up. Quit sending me shit. I'll be fine. I found my key.

O'Brien clapped once, loudly. He hopped up and opened the fridge. He searched behind the carton of almond milk, the bag of green apples, Greek yogurt containers. "Come on," he said. "One more for the big guy!"

Leon / Kitchen   *"Our Champion"*

I was having seizures then. I'd get real cold and drop and then I wouldn't remember much of it. Sometimes I'd bite my tongue. I had my first one on an active unit just after Sandy left. U4. The inmates huddled around me and after twenty seconds of the radio on my hip being tilted past ninety degrees, the body alarm was triggered. "Can't have you on the units," my captain said. "Can't get rid of you, either." So after sixteen years working the tiers, I was reassigned to the kitchen, where the inmate workers made bologna sandwiches and BBQ rib patties.

It was dinnertime, and plating was about to begin on the waterlogged yellow food trays. I could already taste the left-overs I'd put aside. Only a few hours were between a silent basement and me. I stood off in the corner in my food-stained white button-down, black-and-white-checkered pants. Barker House's first cook, long retired, chose the getup. A Vietnam vet who said he wore something similar in a breakfast hall at Da Nang Air Base.

If I were still upstairs, I'd have the inmates locking down for chow. I always gave them a good fifteen minutes in their cells before dinner. It settled their nerves. Late in the afternoon, as another day off their sentences closed, the inmates could get excited. But down here, I supervised the making of chow. Inmates—men convicted of drunken driving, parole violation, loitering—wore steel mesh gloves and chopped carrots with sharp chef's knives, the knife handles connected to a ten-inch chain looped to a ring in the countertop.

Meatloaf was on the menu, seasoned by industrial-sized seasoning packets—*sacks*, a better word. The salty loaf was not the mixture of seasonings I would have used at home—dried mustard the headliner. I used to cook dinner at home even before Sandy's big break, as she called it. She was profiled in *New Hampshire* magazine as a Remarkable Woman of 2007. The top home seller at her agency. A recent Bay State Marathon finisher. But it wasn't the profile that changed her. It was the attention her photo received. Sandy in a black dress, her hands on her hips, standing victorious in front of a SOLD sign. Her trainer said she looked powerful. Facebook comments from strange men: *Gorgeous! Stunner! Me likey likey.* Sandy began weighing her food on a scale before she ate it. If she wasn't at the gym or working, she was running. I didn't mind cooking. When Joey was really small and Sandy was a stay-at-home mom, her dinners were pre-made or packaged. Hamburger Helper or

frozen fried chicken and canned green beans. But I missed her
at the table.

I checked the boiling carrots. The inmate stirring the pots
had his mouth open, his eyes fixed on the bubbling water. He
was leaning toward the pot, and I was afraid he was going to
dunk his face in it. I got close to him and smelled the alcohol,
not booze, but chemical, like hand sanitizer. And then I realized the entire kitchen staff seemed different. Along the
assembly line they laughed, roughhoused, and some yelled
loudly over the hip-hop on the old boom box. I could sometimes trust them too much and forget. I guessed they'd cooked
a batch of apple hooch inside a trash bag, stashed underneath
dirty uniforms in housekeeping. It'd had to be cooking for a
while.

I found Copley struggling with a stack of food trays.

"Are you straight?"

"I'm not gay," he said without looking up from his duty.
Copley's story as told by Copley: I bought a dirt bike off my boy
Rawls for sixty bucks and the thing's a piece of shit. I stick it
under my mom's porch and forget about it. A month later I
enlisted and blah blah blah I do all this shit. You know. I'm over
there for whatever. Eight months. The day I come back they're
waiting for me. Arrest me for stolen property. For a dirt bike
that don't even work.

Copley had told of his plight one night after he'd volunteered
to scrub the meat freezer. We'd sat and ate a tub of sun butter
and a loaf of bread in the pantry afterward.

"I mean sober," I said. "Are you sober?"

"I'm not a rat," said Copley. "And I'm not drunk."

On one side of the counter were five industrial ovens cooking the meatloaf. Two older inmates at the head of the counter smeared pieces of white bread with a scant amount of golden margarine to round out dinner. The other side of the counter was a caravan of metal food carts, ready to be filled with trays and lids, crates of milk cartons, and sent up the elevator to the units.

Copley had a shaved head, patches of red whiskers sticking out in no particular pattern on his zit-scarred face. He removed trays from one of the dishwashers and stacked them on the ground. I could feel the warmth of the dishwasher, the moisture rising up between Copley and me.

I didn't drink. Never had. Sandy didn't either. Our leisure activity was going out to eat. A thing of ours was to try chicken wings from different restaurants. I'm not sure how it began, but we ate chicken wings from Northern New Hampshire down to Cape Cod. The best, we agreed, were the tiki-style wings at T-Bones in Hudson. But then the obsessive running began in correlation with the pre-crash competitive housing market. She lost weight and I could see the muscle in the back of her arms. I didn't like the changes, but Sandy had a way of making me feel like I was making a big deal out of things. "It's not a big deal," she said.

Copley continued to slot the trays but there were only a few left in his stack. I bent at my knees, my fat stomach between my legs, and hoisted a tall, heavy stack of trays off the ground and strained while walking them to the plating station. I left the stack on the station and the inmates who were buttering the bread plated the bread and slid the trays down the line.

I went back to Copley and he was making another stack. I was out of breath and trying to hide it, slowing my breathing. I was embarrassed about my weight gain. The photo ID clipped to my shirt portrayed a different man, with a chin and neck and cheekbones. A man who could keep a wife, or easily find a new one, if he wanted. I used to shave every day back then. I said, "I know they're drunk. But what'd they drink?"

"You look tired, boss," he said. "Go get yourself a cup of coffee."

"Don't tell me what to do." I feigned being strict, but I wasn't. "Sorry." I needed the inmates to have an investment in me. If my brain exploded and I cracked my head, I needed a kind heart to call it in.

"I'm just saying maybe you go and start a pot of coffee."

I counted filled dinner trays on U8 and U9's rolling food cart. After a tip, you needed to continue your duties. I was good with the inmates, especially since I'd traded my pepper spray for a ladle, but they thought I was an incompetent amateur. Fat-ass cook. They'd say, "Leon, the COs are cocksuckers. You boys with them? Nah, Leon ain't. He's on the level." They hadn't known me prior to the weight gain, a side effect of Keppra, and Sandy leaving, and the sleepless nights with Joey's knees jammed in my back. I'd wondered if the seizures were self-punishment. I could beat myself up sometimes and say I deserved them. I welcomed them. When I'd awaken in a spell at home I'd turn the stove on then off, flick the light, open and close the fridge, plate the table then put the plates away, mess with the pans, fill the sink then drain it, look out the window at the empty yard. I'd do this for about twenty minutes until I was done acting normal but in fact was back to normal. When I'd realize Joey hadn't witnessed it, I was elated.

"Your brain may be misfiring" was all I got from the neurologist. If he were more comforting and less unaffected by the news, or possible news, I would have told him about the separation, how the seizures coincided with my wife's leaving.

Dinner went smoothly. The inmates kept the radio loud and the banter crude and racist and it only brought on more laughter. Before I instructed them to commence cleanup, I put three untouched trays from U10's returned food cart inside the pantry. Then I went behind the line of food carts, through the trash receptacle that smelled of meatloaf and soured milk, where the scraps from dinner filled the heap of bags, down the quiet hallway, and into the housekeeping room. Four inmates wearing white T-shirts and tan pants were huddled around the coffeepot in the corner. The large washing machines, six feet high and wide, sloshed netted laundry bags in soapy water. The dryers hummed and rocked loud, muting conversation. They stared at me. I didn't belong there.

"Everyone, away from the coffee."

I didn't know their names. They put their heads down and spread out but didn't stray too far from the coffee maker. The wall opposite the washers and dryers had a metal rack filled with folded uniforms and underneath on the floor were sneakers without laces. The room smelled of mildew and burnt hair. The inmates wouldn't look my way. I was larger than any of the four, height and weight. My legs had become thick and my arms as well; I didn't feel any stronger. I approached the coffee maker and the inmates spread out a bit more. One inmate, a black man with a dark birthmark on his face that looked like Florida, began folding clothes near the rack. I put my nose into the reservoir of the coffee maker and got a whiff of mint.

"What is this?" I asked, holding the coffeepot, a thick, clear liquid covering the bottom.

No one answered. Another inmate started emptying clothes from a dryer into a basket on wheels.

"Who wants to lose good time over this?" Again no answer. I turned to the inmate pretending to fold clothes. "What is this?"

"I didn't drink none of it," he said. "They did. Ask them."

"I'll have everyone put to a hearing."

No one answered. I was breathing quickly and holding the entire Mr. Coffee machine, wrapping the cord around the base.

"Fine," I said, sweating, my collar and my lower back damp. "Everyone against the wall."

The inmates lined up against a free part of the wall, their hands against the white concrete, legs spread, chins down. I held the coffeepot. I'd been letting things go. Everything kept getting farther and farther away from me.

Before a seizure, I'd get really cold. It felt like a chill, one that crept up on you lying in bed, or washing dishes, just a shiver.

But the chill didn't shake a limb. It'd lay me down and take minutes from me. It'd put me on the moon.

I wasn't cold but I was worked up, another warning sign. I stared at the washer, focused on an orange shirt with black lettering, and followed it from the front to the top, and then it disappeared, and after a moment came back again. I didn't know how long I followed the shirt. If I collapsed, I'd be alone. I could die right there and they'd watch me. They'd laugh. They'd finish folding the clothes before telling anyone. They didn't know they had this power over me. I put the coffee maker on the floor and patted each inmate down, handed them their ID tags from the hooks on the wall, and relieved them of their shift. None of them thanked me.

In the kitchen, I waited for cleanup to finish. I lined up my crew outside the elevators, patted them down, too. A normally quiet inmate slapped me on the back. He had a wide smile as he entered the elevator.

Afterward, inside the pantry, I spooned three trays' worth of meatloaf into a metal bowl. I covered it in ketchup and ate it while reading the ingredients on the back of a box of breadcrumbs.

AT FORTY-FIVE, THE backseat of a taxi was a good place to evaluate things. Driving the same way I'd driven home for sixteen years, only now as a passenger, and having to pay for it, made me want to run away like Sandy had. Or sleep. But I could never sleep. Route 3 at eleven thirty at night was quiet and dark but not dark enough. The driver was usually Juan or Benji or sometimes Frank and I'd talked with them enough the first few months to where we didn't need to talk anymore. They knew the state had revoked my license for six months and then extended the revocation. My doctor wasn't confident. I might still have a seizure while driving. I didn't feel them coming on with enough warning, so I wasn't so sure either. I didn't want to kill anyone, or myself.

We had a small house in Concord. A two-bedroom Cape with one bathroom. I got home from work and hoped the inmates went to bed without issue. I showered and ate a ham sandwich on the bed and watched Joey climb a mountain in a blizzard. Joey played this one medieval video game that I hooked up to the bedroom TV. He'd stay up until I got home from work, late, and I'd let him finish whatever quest he was on. His grades disappointed, which was different from when Sandy was here. But it wasn't like Sandy sat down with him and did homework. It'd been years since that. Joey was just going through an ordeal. I'd tell the teachers, "His mother left. He's taking it badly." And they were mostly women and they'd nod and make sad faces and sometimes they'd touch my shoulder. I wondered if they'd seen me climb out of a cab outside the school.

Anyway, his character, Dzole, was in search of a Hagraven, he explained. A witch that was half bird, half woman. "Her talons are poisonous, Dad. It took me an hour to make enough serum to fight her." Joey wore a black hoodie and plaid pajama pants and sat at the edge of the bed with his legs crossed. Dzole, a hardy Nord, was a witch hunter. It was a role-playing game. You got a base character in a lore-heavy world, then imagined who your character was within that world. Excitedly, Joey read me the bio he wrote for Dzole from a message board. It was something like, "Some years ago, while on a job escorting a caravan to Whiterun, his wife and newborn son were kidnapped and used in a sacrificial ceremony by Forsworn witches. Dzole returned to an empty cabin, and with revenge in his blood he set off to destroy unholy creatures, demons, and witches. He would never be satisfied. No amount of money or bounty would fill his heart again. The days were long, for Dzole yearned for the night, when the ones he sought were lurking."

Other kids, adults too, shared their character's stories and the community rated them. Joey's had more thumbs up than down. I understood the need for escape. The need to pretend. I'd been following Joey and Dzole's quests for a few months. I was surprised at how invested I'd become. I watched the Nord's progression from unskilled swordsman to master killer.

Dzole was muscular and wielded a hand ax, wore a leather skirt and a metal helmet with horns. The soundtrack was always impressive, but during a quest, with enemies nearby, the music was epic. The snow fell at a greater speed the farther up the mountain he climbed. The score picked up. I stopped eating my sandwich. A cry, like a crazed eagle, avalanched down the mountain. Joey jumped and paused the game. He put his head down and took a deep breath. I put the plate on the bed and scooted toward him; my body lopsided the mattress. Joey leaned into my weight. He caught himself on my thigh. He was skinny, his fingers piercing. I wished I could give him my fat.

"I'm not ready," he said. His hair covered his ears and, if he let it, his eyes.

"You got this. You said you stocked up. I've seen you fight *dragons*."

He un-paused the game and the cry finished its descent. He continued his climb. The cries got louder but Dzole wasn't afraid.

"The bird woman must die," I said.

She stood on a rock in the distance, her figure hunched, but I couldn't see her face. The dim lamp on the bedside table was drowned out by the glare of the box TV. A gray aura created a funnel in the small room. We were entranced. I couldn't see Sandy's empty white dresser, the one we'd put together on a snowy Saturday morning years ago as Joey lay on a blanket on the floor. I couldn't see my mother's oak rocking chair, the one Sandy had rocked Joey in, nursed him in. The wooden cross above the TV wasn't ours. The blue-veined floral comforter wasn't for two men to sleep under. Dzole didn't move.

"Go get her."

"No," Joey said. "I'm not ready."

"What's the point of playing, then?"

"I'm going to level up some more."

I scooted back to my pillow to finish my sandwich. The bird woman threw a fireball toward Dzole as he jumped off the mountain.

———————————

I HAD SEIZURES in my sleep. After Sandy left, Joey started sleeping in my bed. He said he hadn't seen me have a seizure. But I wasn't sure how he hadn't. I'd wake up and my body would be right up against his. At fourteen, he was almost as tall as me. But if I blanketed his body I'd smother him. I'd crush him. It wasn't safe, what we were doing. We slept like there was a wall between us, or another body. We'd never talked about it, but I knew he didn't want to find himself snuggled up against his father. But he couldn't be alone. Not yet.

In the dark of the bedroom, I'd awoken once damp and stiff, my muscles aching. A small pool of blood on the pillow, and when I touched my wet face, the blood was up into my ear. I wondered if my brain had finally found a way out, spilled onto the pillow. I turned and saw Sandy. She was asleep. I wanted to whisper in her ear to stay, explain to her that the universe had turned on me. We joked, long ago, "Life has no meaning. This is all so silly." And we laughed. It was too easy. The way it all fit in. Then later, in that other life, she said, "Happiness isn't real." I hated her then for being so concise.

I'D NEVER HAD a seizure in public, but I wanted to. The more I thought about the seizures, or willing one on, the less likely I was to have one. It'd been seven months. I'd had seven seizures. I knew my seizures didn't understand time, but I couldn't help but think they were falling into a pattern. Still, they seemed to hit when I'd forgotten about them completely. In line at Subway, surrounded by other customers, waiting for my roast beef sandwich, I wanted to have one. At the bank. In the back of a cab. In the cereal aisle while reaching for Tastee-Os. I wanted to wake up and see worried faces, people on their phones, a kind woman holding the back of my head and asking me if I was okay.

I did try to find Sandy a few weeks after she left. I searched Facebook but she'd deleted her account. I called the Remax office she worked out of, but Meg, the receptionist and her running partner, told me Sandy quit. "Where is she?" I asked. Meg told me she didn't know. I told her I wasn't well. She said sorry. I thought it was a genuine sorry.

I called Sandy's mom in Saratoga.

"She wants to be on her own, Leon," her mother told me. "Respect her wishes."

"Sandy has responsibilities. Your grandson needs his mother."

"She's not good for him right now. He has you."

"I'm not well."

"I'm sorry to hear."

Neither of them took my calls after a few months of check-ins. Her mother sent Joey a birthday card in March. She signed it *Grandmammy XOXO*. There was a check for twenty dollars.

People said sorry a lot. I didn't necessarily dislike the sorrys but I didn't need them. I needed Sandy back. I needed her to fix Joey. I needed my brain back. A sorry was reassurance things weren't getting better. They were getting worse.

I TOLD THE kitchen crew that if they were going to drink during their shifts, they needed to be smarter about it. "Hickey drinks coffee from that thing," I said. Hickey was the part-time cook on my two days off. I searched online and found an easier way to extract alcohol from hand sanitizer.

"Kids do it," I told the two bakers. "Mix the salt in. Let it sit."

Inside the pantry, the bakers—an old, dirty vagrant and a long-haired gay kid—started doling out shots an hour into their dinner shifts. The pantry was near the walk-in freezer at the farthest end of the basement.

I allowed two shots each, which they slurped off a plastic spoon. I read about kids dying from the stuff, so I monitored the shots and made sure no one was fall-down drunk. It was enough to take the edge off and for them to be sober before the shift ended. Even Copley came into the pantry for shots. I received many thank-yous and handshakes and "You don't know what this means to us" but no "I'm sorrys." Dinner and cleanup ran the same as it did before. But I felt safer. I'd begun to want to have a seizure in the kitchen.

JOEY WOULDN'T FIGHT the Hagraven.

"I need to get Dzole to level thirty first," he said one day during breakfast.

I should've been asking about homework and studying. But I was more concerned with his avoidance of the Hagraven. "Do bosses have levels?"

He finished chewing his cereal before he answered. We ate a lot of cereal. "She's level eleven."

"Destroy her, then." I made coffee and filled a bowl of cereal for myself. Joey didn't respond. "Show me how to play. I'll fight her for you."

"You'll die."

"Can't you just restart if you die?"

"Dzole has never died."

That night, Joey sat crisscrossed on the edge of the bed; a big can of energy drink was on the carpet. The living room looked big without a TV. But we really only used half of the house. I wanted to lay on the sectional in the living room, in the dark, and pretend Sandy had come home and taken Joey to wherever it was she went. I wanted that more than I wanted Sandy to come home and stay.

"Did you do it?" I asked as I took off my socks.

"No."

I got in the shower. My stomach was flabby. It wasn't the kind of stomach some men can get away with, tight and round. It was just fat and fleshy. If Sandy walked in and saw me washing under my breasts, she'd gasp. That was the last thing I thought about, Sandy walking in, her hands on her beautiful face, long red nails up near her eyes, shocked and maybe afraid at how fast I'd deteriorated, and then I opened my eyes and Joey was standing over me holding a towel. He was crying. He was spectral, a fuzz emanated off his body.

"You're bleeding."

I was embarrassed, like I'd been caught in a lie. I couldn't move. Blood-tainted water ran under my body toward the drain. The shower curtain was across my legs, plastic rings broken in pieces on my stomach.

I could feel my body loosening. My jaw unhinged. "Can you turn off the water?"

I was bleeding from the back of my head. Joey wasn't crying anymore. He handed me the towel and pulled the shower curtain off me. "I'm okay," I said. "It's just a cut."

"I heard you fall. I heard it happen."

"Did you see it?"

"No. It was over when I came in."

"Good." I stood up with my back to Joey and wrapped the towel around my waist. I felt like I normally did after a seizure. I felt out of body. There was no pain. The blood meant nothing.

"Are you scared?" He started to cry again but quietly. He was wearing his youth baseball jersey from before he quit last season. The Cincinnati Reds. It was bigger on him now than when he played. How'd I let him get so thin? He had his mother's nose, slim with a slight hook at the tip.

"I'm scared all the time."

"I want to help you," he said, and picked up my clothes. He looked exhausted. He handed me my boxers and turned away, looking at the door. I couldn't get my feet off the floor.

"Dad," he said.

"You need to sleep in your own bed."

He was quiet. And then, "Can we talk about this later?" He tossed the rest of my clothes into a pile on the bathroom floor and went to leave.

"Joey," I said, "what if the Hagraven was the one who stole Dzole's family?"

"She wasn't the one," he said, and left.

I opened the medicine cabinet and took out my toothbrush and wet it, then applied toothpaste and then I washed the toothpaste off. I put the toothbrush back. I dried the shower walls with the towel. I took the top off the toilet and adjusted the ball float. I stood in the shower and looked out into the night through the blinds. I tried to find the moon, something I knew was real. I couldn't. But the maroon fence was still there, and so was the birdfeeder we'd hung from an oak branch. Everything was still here. I couldn't see the cut in the mirror because it was right in the center of the back of my head. I rinsed the blood off my hair in the sink and got dressed. From the medicine cabinet, I took Sandy's razor, nail file, contact solution, mouthwash, makeup remover, and floss, and I threw it all in the trash can. I went down the hall and checked on Joey. He was back at his post, the joysticks tapping, buttons clicking.

"You want to talk?" I asked him.

"There's a note from my teacher you need to sign," he said without looking away from the TV. He had it folded on the bed.

It was the usual note he'd been receiving. This one was from Miss Descoteaux. *Your son didn't complete the semester project. He's been sleeping in class. Would you like to chat on the phone or could you come to the school? We can set up a conference. You should come in, Mr. Gomes.*

"I don't want to talk about it."

I put the note on the nightstand and lay on the bed. It felt good to stretch out. I'd be sore in the morning.

"I've been messing up at work, too," I said. Joey clicked the buttons on the controller. I realized Dzole was making the summit to the Hagraven. "Sometimes we get in ruts, Joey. It happens. We need to snap out of it."

"Is she ever coming back?"

"You should prepare like she isn't."

The bird woman screamed. Dzole reached the top of the mountain. He pulled a battle-ax off his back and stood in a fighter's stance, two hands on the handle. Fireballs rained down on him. Joey paused the game. He left the bed and stood in front of the TV. I couldn't see beyond him. By the back of his shirt, I yanked him onto the bed and the controller fell to the floor. Joey looked at me like he had in the bathroom. I wanted to tell him there was no reason to be scared. Before I could, he picked the controller back up and ran Dzole toward the fire slinger.

DON: I have this dog that likes to eat tuna. I feed the cat then that big fucking lab ass-bumps her into the other room and eats her food.

RAY: I had a dog when I was a kid. Ran away. Hit the light, Don, I'm done reading.

DON: I started feeding him cat food, then I found that light tuna shit to be cheaper. He looks healthy. Better than he ever has.

RAY: You got to really smack it. The side there. Button's jammed.

DON: Bernie. The dog's name is Bernie.

RAY: . . .

DON: Seven years of the dry food crap and he starts eating tuna and looks great. His nose doesn't have crusties and his nails, Jesus, those nails could cut through the visiting glass. I called my daughter, she's staying there till I get out and she tells me he won't eat the tuna. Her tone. Like I made it up.

RAY: Don, I'm tired.

DON: She says there's a mound of stinking fucking fish in his bowl and now what's she supposed to do. I told her keep feeding him the tuna. If he's hungry he'll go for it.

RAY: Sure.

DON: She tells me I'm crazy. I belong in jail. But that's where she's wrong. Jail ain't supposed to be for crazy. She might be right about the tuna though.

RAY: You got yourself a smart one.

DON: She didn't get it from her mother. That whore couldn't spell *tuna.* Anyways, I wrote her last night and told her to get rid of the both of them. The cat and Bernie. Looks like my lawyer isn't too excited about my trial. I was thinking plea deal but I'm too old for plea deals. I'll put your glasses on for the trial. Can I borrow your glasses? I'll act like I'm drooling and falling asleep and I'll stick those big fucking beer mugs on my face like I'm retarded or something.

RAY: Where's Bernie going to go?

DON: Hell if I know. Maybe right back where I got him. I ever tell you about my sister, Maple? Sure, I have. Maple found that dog on her property in Milford. She phoned me and told me I might like him. He was ugly, like me. First I saw

him he was roped outside in the rain. I felt for the old guy,
how couldn't I? The way his legs shaked when he pissed.
I don't look it but I can be a big softy, Ray.

RAY: . . .

DON: Ray?

H e is interested in Inmate Jakobens for no other reason than he is bored and Jakobens is in front of him. Jakobens sits at a dayroom table on the left bottom tier near the running showers. He is older, maybe the oldest inmate on the medium security unit. Even with three squares a day, Jakobens is built like a flyweight. His eyes are black under his white brows. He is watching the large flat-screen mounted high on the blue brick wall. Dixon's genius idea of painting the units soothing colors made the jail into a kiddy camp. Gone were the gray and steel. In came the cameras, the rainbow-colored walls, the pussification of a once feared jail where Menser had been proud to thump bigmouthed inmates. The old man seems to be enjoying the décor. Menser sidles up next to him and watches a few minutes of *The Sopranos* and laughs when he feels like he should. Jakobens ignores him. Menser plays with his noose knife, the tool he's used twice to cut down swingers. One died, one lived. He flicks the sharp J-hook open with his thumb, then presses the rounded edge on his thigh and closes it. Flicks it open, closes it. The old man pays him no attention. Menser asks him what he thinks of Tony banging his psychiatrist.

"You don't remember me from Max," says Jakobens. "Do you?"

"I don't."

"I asked you for a blanket for four days," Jakobens says as he turns his attention back to the TV. "You kept telling me you'd get me one." His thin legs are crossed and his hairy hands grip the heel of his resting foot. "I timed out before ever getting one."

"Tough luck." Menser can't remember the man or the request. Blankets are hard to come by in the winter. Too bad. "Has Big Pussy died yet?"

"What?" asks Jakobens, turning back to Menser.

Menser steps away, walks along the top tier, breathes through his mouth so he can't smell the inmates shitting in their cells, or the bad breath. It seems everyone has bad breath. He tries to show a young Cambodian inmate in the weight area how to do leg presses with the chest machine. Menser gets on his back, positions his boots under the metal bar, but gets stuck. He struggles to get back up.

"Damn," the kid says, "I thought cops were the only pigs that ate doughnuts." The half dozen inmates in the weight area laugh. Menser wants to say it's not the doughnuts he eats so often, it's the kid's mother's fuck box. But he can't get it out. Instead he grunts.

His boots are jammed, his knees pressed against his belly, his large body stuck under the weight of the plates. The blood rushes to his head, the orange jumpsuits beginning to close on him, their laughter wild, and he flails his arms on the cold hard floor. If he can get to his feet, he thinks, he can take all of them, but he knows they won't fight an officer like him fairly. He wiggles his right boot off and that gives him enough room to roll onto his side. The yelling and laughter must have caught Brenner's attention, because she arrives and helps him to his feet. He waves her off and goes to his boot.

"Clear out!" Brenner yells to the inmates on the mezzanine, her voice feminine but surprisingly effective. Menser sticks his foot into his boot. "It's enough running this unit by myself," she says. "I don't know what to do with you."

"I don't need you to do anything with me."

Brenner's black hair is pulled back tightly, showing every inch of skin on her face. She has fat dark freckles that look like holes on a dartboard. Menser wants to criticize her. But Brenner is attractive. He can't think of what to insult her about. "I'm fine," he tells her instead.

Menser decides to find a corner to stand in. He backs himself in near the rec yard door underneath the mezzanine, where he can observe the inmates in the dayroom, a sliver of the come-filled shower stalls, the filing-cabinet officer station Brenner stands at, the sally port, the pay phones, and if he gets ambitious enough to mosey over to the rec yard door, the rec yard. He watches inmates gamble future canteen on cards and air-hump Brenner's ass as she walks by. He studies the inmates as they hurry by him, gathering cheese-sauce packets and nachos to bring back to their holes. The Puerto Ricans clutter the tables with dominoes. The old-timers watch TV while comfortably drugged, like it's a goddamn nursing home. The shift passes. He may have dozed off at one point. The inmates circle the unit in a swirl of small movements, handshakes, nods, fingers carefully remembering phone numbers from the real world. They laugh and rap in the shower. Weight stacks crash above. The caged clock ticks the shift away. Menser hates their smiles, their existence. He wants them to be hurting. He is thirty-six, nine years into his own twenty-year sentence, with high blood pressure, unmarried. It occurs to him that there's a carelessness that comes with the orange jumpsuit. A weight lifted. He decides to make a round and hopes one of the pissants asks how his mom is doing.

———————

MENSER HAS LIVED in the same eight-hundred-square-foot single family home in Nashua his whole life. He mows the lawn with a plug-in electric mower that smells like it burns the lawn instead of cuts it. He buys wood for the stove from Marty's Lumber in Hudson. His father used to cut the wood himself and weed-whack around the mailbox. High grass covers the pole of the mailbox now. Trivial chores his father had the luxury of doing. They pale in comparison with having to supervise Menser's mother, so he doesn't care the neighbors are sure to notice his failings in his father's absence. The same contractor built the dead-end street's eight homes in the forties, all identical in structure, plain, on ten-thousand-square-foot lots. The happy neighbors have loud children, triangular hydrangeas, basketball hoops, and walkways lined with freakishly large hostas.

He gets home from his shift that day and his mother, Fay, is asleep in her gray leather chair. Her left arm is slung over the armrest, which is zigzagged with burn holes. Her body is drooped. Menser asked her to comb her hair this morning, but she never does, and he can see the bald spots among the white. The TV is loud, three judges in robes yell at a man holding a poodle. His mother is deaf and watches the TV with the volume on 84. He turns it down.

He goes to her room and strips her bed to wash the piss out of the sheets. He groans, blows air out of his nostrils as he passes her in her chair, holding the sheets in front of him. The groan goes unnoticed. Sometimes he forgets she is deaf, she is gone. He goes into the basement with the sheets, moves the wet clothes from the washer to the dryer, then fills the washer with the soiled sheets. Back upstairs, his mother is now awake, the volume turned back up to 84.

"Did you bathe today?" he asks her. He rubs his hair and body like he is rinsing off soap.

She waves him off. He goes down the hallway to the bathroom. The tub is dry. He sometimes sneaks behind her and smells her but today he's not in the mood.

He could never have imagined having to bathe her, fix her meals, make sure she was wiping after she shit. She had been a good mother growing up. He was an only child, and she had treated him like a gift from God. She'd called him that, long ago, one night after a Boy Scouts meeting as he sat at the dinner table, trying to replicate a knot they'd learned with a shoelace. "You bring us such joy," she'd said, stirring a pot of sauce. "We tried for years. You came to me after Christmas and your father didn't believe me." His father had never been an optimist. Menser thought him to be an ordinary father. He'd laughed when reading the paper, yelled at the news on the TV. He always walked with his arms tight by his sides and bent and crouched like he had a bad back, but he didn't.

Once, when Menser was twelve, maybe thirteen, his father took him to see a Red Sox game. He remembers the park's stench: peanut shells, steamed hot dogs, stale beer, the sour urine in the trough, his father so close to him in their bleacher seats he could smell him, too. He remembers that aroma, like wood, when he wears his father's postal uniform windbreaker. He misses the woody scent, but only briefly. It was then his father said something important to Menser, something he thinks about often. Not looking at the boy, his father leaned in after a Sox homer and said, "There are moments when I ask myself, if the world were to end now, would it be okay with me." That was as sentimental as the old man got.

This isn't a moment within which Menser would be okay dying. He stares at the linoleum kitchen floor that's peeling in a few spots near the radiator and dishwasher. On breezy days like today, a couple of detached vinyl siding panels outside the kitchen and Menser's bedroom whack against the house. As he microwaves his mother's dinner, he hears the whacking over the appliance's humming, pictures his father say in his Camel-unfiltered voice, "Loose J-channel. Nothing a couple of nails won't fix." Menser won't fix the panels. Instead, he walks by them, watches them flap. At night, he falls asleep to the rhythmic sound.

They eat in the kitchen at a round table kitty-corner in front of the only window in the room. Figurines of blue jays are scattered on shelves, in a glass case above the light switch, magnets of blue jays on the fridge, yellowing, sliding down slowly. Menser takes out the Lean Cuisine from the microwave and opens it in front of her, steaming and salty. He shoves a fork into her permanently clenched right hand and starts her first mouthful, reminding her of what she is doing. Slowly, she chews and some macaroni falls out of her mouth. He watches her face muscles labor. She holds the fork and stares at the jug of stale protein powder atop the fridge.

"Take another bite," he says and raps the table. She doesn't even blink. "I'm not feeding you the whole damn thing." He raps the table again. He wants to rip the fork from her and stab her cheek straight through her tongue, out the other cheek, kabob her face, make her look him in the eye. He grabs her hand and she jolts but doesn't pull away. He guides the fork into the warm macaroni. She doesn't take the bite. He stands.

"Please eat." He smooths her hair away from her face, holds it in a bunch behind her head with one hand, and feeds her.

After dinner, Menser lets his mother work her way back to her chair. He makes her a highball before she points to her glass. Then he puts the bottle of gin and a liter of tonic water on the floor next to her chair. Menser shuffles out before she needs another one and leaves her to smoke half a pack of Misty menthols. He undresses, looks through the pile of clothes on the edge of his bed for sweatpants, a cutoff T-shirt he likes to wear on arm days. He can't find either. In his boxers, he sits on the bed. Outside, dusk moves in. It is days before Halloween, the New England nighttime impatient, the backyard absent of anything that moves. His room is quiet. His useless phone without messages. He types out a Facebook post: *gyming it. pipes day.* He leaves the post up for a few minutes, scrolls through his news feed. Everything is fake. He doesn't like any pictures. He likes a life-hack post claiming vodka tightens your pores. He checks his status. No likes, so he deletes it. He goes over his day, remembering the incident at the weights. He feels bad for not thanking Brenner, but how could he? His mother yells and he runs from his room to find her asleep, making tiny screams. He squishes her cigarette in the ashtray and mutes the TV.

HE WATCHES BRENNER prance around and he swears she knows the inmates are wagging their tongues at her. The more he watches her, the more he wants her to get pushed into a cell by a couple of them, teach her not to tease the animals.

The inmates ignore him. He is tired. He makes a round of the two-tiered unit, up the east stairwell, bangs his boots on the metal stairs. Dominoes clap. He gloves up and slides into an unoccupied cell and sits at the desk stool. The unit's sounds echo off the bare walls. He treats it like a breakroom. In the cell to the left, there's these two inmates who argue and joke and tell stories and Menser likes to listen to them. They call each other by their first names and there's something reassuring about that. Don and Ray. But they're quiet today. Outside the cell, Inmate Jakobens, with his long white hair tied up in a girlish bun, stands at the top of the stairs and picks a scab on his forehead. He asks Menser for the time.

"It's ten twenty," Menser says, reading off his black plastic wristwatch.

"The hour of the gods."

"What?"

"The beginning of afternoon. I love the afternoon," says Jakobens.

Menser keeps on, but Jakobens catches up. A telephone is slammed onto its receiver below and a fat inmate screams *you fucking whore* into a dead phone. Brenner heads over. Menser moves across the top tier, peers into cells, while Jakobens mimics his movements.

Menser says, "Fuck off, *in*mate." He stops and looks over the railing to check on his partner, but she has it under control. The fat inmate is seated on a stool at a dayroom table, with Brenner counseling him, standing over him. Poor body language, poor positioning.

Jakobens stops with him and glares over the railing, his eyes tiny, the whites reddish like chicken eyes. "Some men can't keep control of their women while they're away," he says.

"What cell is yours?" Menser asks.

Pointing down to the west bottom tier, where a group of inmates play three-card poker, Jakobens says, "Twenty-three nineteen."

"Your cell is down there, but you're hanging around on the mezzanine."

"Perspective."

Menser nods and continues his round. "You shouldn't hang around on the mezzanine." The word stock and straight from the handbook. *Mezzanine.* If asked to define, Menser wouldn't articulate it well. A porch, a landing, a floor above another floor.

"You're going through a change," says Jakobens. "There's something about this jail that is different than other jails I've been in. You guys are clean, tidy, put together. But I can't figure you out. You look terrible."

Menser stops walking. "So do you." He tucks in his shirt, the texture papery, like a brown bag, the color, too.

"You're at the end of something," Jakobens says and then puts his thin forearms on the top railing and looks out again at the dayroom below. "When people go through a transition, there's an obvious death then a rebirth, or just a death, but it's evident there's a change happening."

"You don't know me."

Jakobens's eyes are close together, his face oddly narrow, disappointed, and he says, "I've known you longer than you've known me."

"You go around telling everyone this? Try to get a rise out of them?"

"No." He picks at the scab, an overworked pimple maybe, and it comes off. He looks at the dried blood. "You're exploding. You're at the end of the world."

HE SITS AT the stool in Jakobens's cell, scanning through Jakobens's legal work. From where he sits, to his right is a blue metal bunk bed, both beds covered in worn gray blankets. Underneath are their property boxes, big toilet paper boxes cut horizontally, then filled with snacks, hot sausage, chips, and torn paperbacks. In front of him near the door are the toilet and sink fixture, above bolted into the wall a dented plastic mirror. Attached to the stool where he sits is a desk, with two cubbies, one for each inmate in the cell, which is usually filled with photos, mail, and legal papers, sealed in manila envelopes. Above him, a weak bulb, blurred behind heavy Plexiglas. Miniature figurines rest on the desk: a hot rod, a woman's legs, and an open book, sculpted from bars of soap. Menser has never seen something like that in the jail. There is artistry to it. He guesses it's been done with a razor blade, and though probably an infraction, he lets them stay. He goes back to scanning Jakobens's legal work.

A list of charges on a docket sheet. Trial date. Sixteen counts of sexual assault on a minor. False imprisonment. Kidnapping. Menser stares at the air vent above the mirror, listens to the heat pushing through, fighting through the tiny holes not plugged with toilet paper balls. He tucks the legal sheets back into the envelope and in his large hands he squishes the figurines, starting with the woman's legs, until they become just soap again, and leaves the crumpled remains.

He moves his attention to the tall stack of letters in the desk. Beginning with the one on top, he reads the handwritten letter, in wild writing, every word a different size, with poor spelling and grammar, hearts above lowercase *i*'s, words scribbled out, lines of anger and hate then love and longing in succession like different women had written each line. *You're the worst father. She adores you . . . You won't be home for Christmas . . . I told you to sell the car . . . You always loved that dress on me. I won't let him fuck me with it on . . . I told Johnny he owes you and that's like owing me.* The words feel real. Jakobens, a skinner, has love. *Hunny when you get out, Cassie is waiting, just like you were her daddy before, you can be again. This is all here still for you. Your kingdom.*

He stands at the tiny cell window overlooking Elm Street outside. He imagines Jakobens's displeasure at having sight of the St. Peter's cemetery littered with flowers and mourners. There's comfort in how painful it is to watch people freely driving by, pulling into the long drive-thru coffee shop line with time to wait, walking their dogs, taking smoke breaks outside the drop-in medical center across Elm. How Jakobens has to watch the snow fall, then melt; the leaves bloom, then die.

———————————

EACH DAY THEREAFTER, he waits until Brenner leaves for change-out details in Booking and returns to Jakobens's cell. He is so interested in the letters he goes back every shift and gets caught up in the ongoing saga, excited when he fingers through the stacks of envelopes and finds one thick with folded pages of love quarrels and cryptic phrases. *She was too young to have a cherry on her sundae.* He isn't so much intrigued by the perversity. What he wants most from them is to learn how a man like Jakobens can find love, tame love, then violate it.

Jakobens's girlfriend, Heather, wrote letters about how much she misses his dick, sprayed the letters with some type of cheap perfume that smells like an energy drink. Menser hates her.

He gets a creeping feeling he's been in the cell too long, but he doesn't want to stop. He gathers up two or three letters he hasn't read yet, older ones from Heather, folds them tightly, and puts them in his back pocket. He's not done this before.

He comes out of the cell and Jakobens sits at the nearest dayroom table and watches him.

"Hey, CO!" Jakobens yells. A common callout. No one stops, the showers run, and the card games go on. Brenner has her head down, writing on top of a filing cabinet.

Menser ducks into the next cell. An inmate is pissing. "Cell search," Menser says. "Screw."

The inmate wiggles and flushes and leaves without a word. Menser goes straight to the stool and sits. He's hot. The folded paper in his back pocket pokes his ass cheek. He misses the distraction the radio traffic brings, tells himself maybe tomorrow he'll take the unit radio from Brenner.

Jakobens appears in the threshold of the cell. With his greasy hair long and flat down over his threadbare shoulders, he looks diseased.

"You destroyed my soap creations," he says. He puts his hands down near his hips like he is searching for pockets that aren't there. "That wasn't nice."

"You're a skinner," Menser says.

"Some do say that."

"Humans say." Menser crosses his feet, his boots heavy, the sweaty socks making his feet itch.

"So judgmental. Tsk-tsk."

Menser rubs his face. "Somebody's going to thump you. Why the fuck aren't you on the skinner pod?"

"I'm protected," Jakobens says. "Pod lawyer. I know important things about things that are important to these boys."

"This place has gone soft," Menser says. "You're disgusting."

"It's poor form to judge what you don't understand."

He tries to strategize a way he can get Jakobens deeper in the cell, out of camera sight. Nothing comes. There's a razor on the sink. He could smash Jakobens's face on the toilet quick, then cut himself to look like it was self-defense. He can't pull it off. "What do you want from them?"

"Simple. They pay me in food."

"Not the inmates, dummy, the kids. What do you want from the kids?"

"Oh, them." Jakobens smiles, his teeth small and coffee-stained. "I want them to feel loved."

Menser stares at Jakobens's slippers. They're dirty, passed down through the House's ages, worn by men better than Jakobens, but also worse. There's no good anywhere. "Come in the cell," Menser says and stands. He brushes his uniform awkwardly because it isn't something he's done before. "Come on."

Jakobens turns on his heels like a dancer and with crossed arms he walks out of sight.

AT NIGHT, MENSER reads the letters in his room. He feels grounded with the letters, Heather's trust, her almost cultish sacrifice of her young daughter, Cassie, and it makes Menser think of his mother differently, as a tragedy, and he begins treating her with more tenderness. The night before, after reading the line *She's part of me, take all of her,* Menser sat with his mother while she watched TV, didn't complain about her smoking her cigarette down until she burnt her fingers, brushed her hair away when she fell asleep, and kissed her wrinkled cheek.

He is sure Jakobens knows about the theft, but he still goes into work with empty sheets of lined paper folded in his pocket so he can fill the next envelope with padded deception anyway, the way an escaped inmate would leave pillows under the bedding to conceal his absence.

Lifting letters isn't exciting. He feels nauseous each time he does it, shook—will sometimes sidle up to Brenner and feel at the letters and try to talk himself into confessing to her right there in the dayroom. She would scold him good, then turn him in to the lieutenant. He'd get what he deserves, a suspension, maybe get coaxed into an early retirement. Brenner would get a good-soldier notch on her belt. The world would center, everyone in their right place. But he gets sudden moments of relief. He becomes anxious and tries to get the feeling of wrong-doing back.

———————————

FAY DIES ON the first Thursday in November, just a week after he began taking the letters. She is in her chair, slouched over an ashtray full of cigarette stubs, the sun late in its morning arrival, beginning to crawl up her peach blouse, just under her flabby chin. A preacher on TV is throwing someone's crutches into a crowd, proclaiming salvation, redemption, healing.

Menser covers her in her Christmas afghan. He sits with her for a while, in his uniform, long enough for the sun to enter the entire room. Not quite saddened, he says an Our Father, holding her hand. Her highball glass has fingerprints on it. Her feet are curled in the carpet. When Menser turns off the TV, he enjoys a good while of silence.

The services are exciting. The officers from Barker House enter orderly, like soldiers. He wants to join the line with them, cross by his mother as though he doesn't know her, just another brother in sequence, honoring a fallen comrade. Brenner shows up and she looks sad to see him. She holds his hand for a moment before Fay's body, and then hugs him. He can feel her breasts against him and doesn't feel ashamed at noticing how soft they are.

He thanks Brenner for coming and doesn't let go of her hand.

She smiles, and with her hair down, her body slender in a black dress, there is no question she is beautiful. "I'm so sorry, Eric."

The sound of his name startles him. Courage comes over him, or impulsivity he is new to, and he says, "After this, you know, the burial. We should go out. Me and you."

Brenner looks at a landscape painting of New England foliage behind him. "I have a lot going on, Eric," she says and lets go of his hand. A cousin and his wife wait in line behind Brenner. Fay's body is within arm's reach.

"I haven't been that nice to you. But that's not me. I'm not bad when you get to know me," he says.

"Not now," Brenner says. "Just not now."

The burly cousin hugs him and says his sorrys but Menser watches Brenner kneel for a moment, sign the cross, and leave the funeral home.

AFTERWARD HE UNDERTAKES the solitary task of boxing up her clothes, figurines, jays, picking what to keep and what to discard. The folding TV dinner stands. The ashtrays. No one will ever occupy her chair again. He carries it to the curb outside. A neighbor, raking leaves, waves sympathetically.

He takes two days off from work and sits in his room and reads over the letters. He memorizes lines: *I feel but a boy. We can make up the time.* He wants back on the tier, inside the cell. For the first time, he tries to picture Heather and Cassie. But he can't imagine them, can't attach images to them. He so badly

wants to. But he can picture the way his mother held her cigarette, the stains in her blouses, how different she was from years
ago, when she kissed his father, spoke to Menser. Her voice was
soothing and peaceful, like the moment before sleep.

FOURTEEN TWELVE ATHENS WAY, Apt. 2, Nashua, NH.
A short drive from his home, so short he feels sickened at the
thought that things like this happen this close to him. Though
he sees offenders each day, there is a strange distance between
their crimes, the victims, and his work. Six rows of bricked,
connected public housing, some with screen doors that don't
seem to close, some with no screen door at all, run vertical on
a large oval of grass and walkways. A few boys ride bikes
through the leaves covering the ground, circle a building, then
emerge from the other side. Menser watches from his truck as
the sun sets behind the first building, between trees, dipping
itself into the Merrimack River. He saves a good amount of
mint tobacco juice in his mouth before spitting it into a coffee
cup. Other than the boys on the bikes, some lights on in
windows, the complex looks deserted. He waits for the boys to
disappear again and then he gets out of the truck.

Wearing his uniform with his badge, to a common person
he resembles any law enforcer. His boots drag through the thick
layer of leaves, his exposed skin cold. The boys come out from
behind the building, but his fear of being stopped or confronted
is gone. He feels like he is doing something right, just plain old
right. He stands in front of the large white numbers, 1412, high

on the corner near the street where he came in, the return address on Heather's letters, and the boys stare. There are four of them. They say something to him but he doesn't hear.

He pounds on the door. A TV is on. A woman speaks Spanish loudly with no response, and he guesses she is on the phone. He holds the screen door open with his hip. There is no intruder light, and behind him the sky is almost dark. The door opens slowly to a living room, with one lamp on, and a small girl looks up at him. Her eyes are soft and black. She is wearing mismatched pajamas, the shirt with pink cupcakes on it, and the bottoms lime green with dinosaurs. She is brown and so small. Behind her a chubby woman leans against the hallway wall with her back to him. He is right—on the phone, waving her free hand. The young girl doesn't smile or move. There is no anticipation in either of them. The boys begin to yell, "What do you want?" "Hey, what's he want?" Menser is flattered by the girl's silence. There is a pang of hopefulness. He doesn't imagine her in the hands of Jakobens then; he hasn't thought of Jakobens since he left his truck. The TV is loud, playing a cartoon. He holds out his hand, and the boys yell "Hey!" forcefully.

"Mom!" the girl cries, and her mother turns to Menser in the doorway.

"What you doing? We ain't done nothing." The woman takes the phone from her mouth and hurries to the door. Menser puts a hand up to her.

"Bullshit," he says, and is, for the first time, aware he has crossed some line.

The woman pushes the girl behind her and gets close to Menser. She is large and animated, waving her hands in his face.

"You ain't a cop," she says, looking at his uniform. "What the hell are you?"

"Your boyfriend, Jakobens. It's sick. All of it."

"That old man? He ain't my boyfriend. He lives down there. I don't know him or give a shit."

Menser tries to see around the woman. He wants to get a look at the girl's face. But the woman pushes him, hard, and he falls off the step. She shuts the door and the boys on the bikes stare at him. He runs toward his truck as fast as he can but it feels like he is moving slowly, the wind filling his lungs with air, his legs heavy, his whole body heavy. Cars drive down the street with their headlights on, pointed at him, music thumping from inside, and he is worried people are watching him, making note of a stupid man in uniform running through the projects. It hits him during his escape that the rescue mission was dumb, and he longs to be in the safety of his bedroom, listening to the laugh track of a sitcom from the living room, the crack of the loose siding outside his window, the smell of cigarettes and the fat envelopes in his hand, the unknown contents exciting and tormenting him. He turns to find nobody chasing him. Menser gets inside the truck and shuts the door but the dome light stays on. He smacks the button and the light goes out so now no one can see him.

Part II

PROPERTY

I made a round of the octagon, a single-tiered unit. I liked how the unit was only one floor. Everything was right in front of me: no stairs or blind spots. The four showers were all in use and I knelt to see under the curtains to make sure only one set of legs was in each stall. Some inmates were watching a reality show on TV. The eighty bunks were half filled. U1 was the only female unit in Barker House: a private jail with a tight budget and strict rules. "I better be able to bounce a quarter on your made bed," I'd say to the inmates. It was an army thing, or something. I wasn't a veteran but I pretended I was when I said things like that.

I'd been on U1 for six months and had the unit running smoothly. They'd flirt with me. I didn't mind the pick-me-up. On visiting days I let them wear eye makeup they'd made from colored pencil shavings. They were the wives and girlfriends

I didn't have, who needed the flirting just as much as they needed the answer no. They demanded my attention as much as the real thing. After punching out each shift, I was drained, like I'd gone a few rounds with a rebellious daughter.

An inmate, with her legs up near her ears, fucked herself with a pink toothbrush container in her cell. I slowed, hung a glance, but kept walking. When I reached Nina's cell I stopped and knocked on the cell door. She lived in a corner cell, so you had to push the swinging door in to enter. I'd assigned her a corner cell when I saw her name. Inmates begged me for those cell assignments. Privacy was something I could give.

I'd dated Nina in eleventh grade. I'd heard she had a kid young but other than that I hadn't given her much thought. When I saw her on my unit two weeks before, leaving the showers with wet hair and braless in a tank top, I was reminded of how she liked getting kissed behind her ears. Nina was just as skinny as ever even after having a kid. She had nice breasts for a skinny girl, a body with all the answers. I couldn't see any track marks or bruises.

We talked during shifts, normal catching-up. She'd gotten into posting crushing ads on Craigslist and had gotten picked up in a prostitution sting at a hotel in Nashua. "Men pay me good money to step on their balls in stilettos," she'd said. "I don't fuck them. But that asshole detective said solicitation is solicitation. My lawyer thinks I have a good case."

I held the steel door open with my shoulder and stood in the threshold of the cell. Nina was lying under the blanket and I could see her bare shoulders, the top of her bare chest. Her desk was covered in letters and envelopes. There was a sliver of daylight coming in through the rectangular window above the desk. Most female inmates tried to spruce up their cells, taping kids' coloring sheets to the walls, collages made from magazine cutouts. They'd rub cocoa butter or lotion on the air vents. But Nina's cell was plain old brick and steel. It smelled like dirty laundry. An officer loudly made a call over the radio, and it echoed through the small cell. I turned my radio off to make certain there wouldn't be an open mic. Some of these guys sat on their radios and the shit they'd let fly had led to fights in the parking lot.

"Feeling better today?" I asked. She'd been depressed, enough that I'd think about her when I was at home while trying to watch the Sox. She slid into a county-issued, yellowish-white tank top.

"Everyone is blind. They walk around smiling. Even you, Mike." There were a lot of philosophers in Barker House.

Nina hadn't been leaving her cell much except to shower. She was trading phone cards for tuna packets and skipping meals.

"There's no right or wrong way to act," I said. "I pretend it's a boardinghouse and you guys are just visitors, waiting for your ride out."

"I wake up and feel sick."

"You won't be here forever." I'd told myself that. I thought maybe when she got out I could help straighten her life out. I hadn't been searching for a girlfriend but I wasn't against having one either. We could date ex-inmates. It was a matter of timing.

"My lawyer sent me a letter. Trial is set for six months from now."

"Six months is cake."

"Maybe, I don't know. I can't turn my mind off, thinking about everything. The past, present, future, it's all bouncing around in this box. And Ava. My mother is going to turn on her soon."

Ava was Nina's daughter. Nina fell for a kid who drove a tow truck and always had cash after high school. Eddie or Frankie. She was back at her mom's, and Eddie or Frankie was long gone.

"You'll survive. So will your mother and Ava."

"It's bad enough that I'm here. But seeing you. You must think I'm the worst." She started to cry. The girls looked occupied with the TV so I went into the cell and sat next to her. I put my arm around her. It was the first time I had embraced an inmate but I didn't feel wrong about it. I'd embraced Nina before, just in another life. She gave herself up and her full weight went into me. She was small in my arms and it brought me back to the backseat of my Mercury Topaz, parked behind Blockbuster.

"You're going to get out," I said. "Your bust is small-scale. And Ava is young. She won't remember all this." I hugged her harder but kept my nose up away from her hair. I knew if I smelled her hair and I liked the way it smelled then I might put myself in a bad situation. She touched the exposed skin on my head and I felt a flutter in my groin.

"She's ten. I remember things from when I was ten. My mother's boyfriend Gabriel—Gabe, he made me call him—and his stupid gold Cutlass," Nina said. "God. She's alone with that bitch. She'll remember."

I wondered if I could remember anything. My first home run. My dad giving me sips of beer after the game while we listened to the Sox on the radio in the backyard. That rusted firepit. Those useless citronella candles my mother swore by. Dad's hair, full and combed. My dog, Fenway, trying to get my game ball.

"I don't remember shit from when I was ten," I said.

"I need a favor." She put her hand on my thigh and she had me; I'd like to think it wasn't as easy as it seemed.

I lowered my nose into her hair. "What do you need?"

THE ONE-STORY SCHOOL was in Milford. It was a string of four gray trailers, small windows up near the roof, and metal ramps running up the doors. They looked new. Students hung around outside the first trailer. I pulled up behind a truck and got out. A girl approached my car.

Ava was taller than I'd expected. I didn't really know how tall a ten-year-old should be. The kid's hair was messy and tangled, and she was missing teeth. She wore a shirt that was too small for her, had a huddle of girls drawn on it in neon colors, goofy monsters lurking behind them. Her pink shorts had pen ink on them near the pockets and she wore black Crocs.

"My mom said to look out for a red Corolla," she said. She circled my car and inspected it like a worried mechanic.

"You don't like my wheels?" After I said "wheels" I felt old. I wouldn't normally say "wheels." "I'm Mike."

"I figured."

She climbed into the backseat. She acted familiar with being picked up from school by a stranger.

"Nobody asked me for ID. There wasn't a teacher. Aren't they supposed to check who picks you up?"

Ava crossed her arms. "The teachers don't give a care here."

"I used to take the bus," I said into the rearview mirror. She looked small with the seat belt high up near her neck. "I loved the bus."

"You can only take it if someone is there to get you off."

"I see."

Nina had asked me to pick up Ava and watch her for a few hours until her grandmother finished her shift at Big Lots. It was two o'clock and hot. I didn't know anything about occupying a kid.

I could have been trying to win Nina over. I always liked being thanked by women.

I drove through the city aimlessly for fifteen minutes and watched as Ava looked out the window, trying to figure out where we were going. Maybe I could feed her. I pulled in to the McDonald's on Bridge Street, with the big slide and ball pit. Ava walked next to me but I kept looking at her to make sure she was still there.

"What are you in the mood for?" I asked. "Double cheese? Chicken nuggets?"

"Oreo McFlurry," she said. She walked away from me and I thought I should stop her. But the dining area only had a few people eating and Ava seemed like she could hold her own.

I ordered our food and brought it to the table. Her eyes were hazel, definitely not Nina's black ones. She licked her spoon and looked uninterested, staring off toward no attractions.

"You can go off in the playground thing," I said. No other kids were in there.

"And get herpes? Um, no."

I ate my burger and tried not to stare. She kept her face turned away, watching a homeless man nodding off in the corner.

"So, your school. What's up with the trailers? They don't have brick schools anymore or buildings?"

"It's a special school," she said. "There aren't a lot of students." After another bite of her McFlurry she said, "Modular."

"What?"

"They're modular buildings. Not trailers."

"Oh."

"Can I have a dollar?" she asked.

"Still hungry?"

She pointed. "It's for that man."

I handed her a dollar and she jumped up and walked over to him, tapped him on the shoulder. He picked his head up slowly. She held the dollar out and he took it. They didn't say a word. She walked back.

"That was nice of you, Ava."

She nodded and scraped the bottom of the cup with her spoon. I wanted to comb her hair.

"How do you know Nina?" she asked, wiggling the spoon between her fingers.

"We dated in high school."

"And now?"

"Your mom reached out to me. She needed help and trusts me."

"How come I never heard of you?"

I didn't answer her. I smiled and looked around the restaurant. An elderly couple sat behind Ava and shared a large fry. Another man sat alone and read the newspaper and drank from a huge cup.

"Is your mom dating anyone?"

"She dates lots of people—guys, girls. She trusts you but you don't even know that about her?"

"Can you give me one name in particular?"

"No. Forget it," Ava said. "Why does she trust you?"

I didn't know how to answer. I couldn't tell her that in desperation we could talk ourselves into trusting almost anyone. "We know a lot about each other," I said. "When you know someone for so long you build trust."

"Tell me something Nina doesn't know about you. Anything."

"Why?"

"So when I tell her about you I can say something she doesn't know." Her McFlurry was finished and her hands were clasped before her on the table. She leaned in.

I thought for a second. "Here's one: I can't pee into a urinal if there's already pee in it."

"Weird." She crunched up her face. "Don't they flush on their own?"

"Some urinals do. Not all."

"That'll freak her out. But, something else."

"That wasn't enough?"

"Nope." Her sharp eyes commanded my attention.

"Okay. My dad has cancer."

"Oh. Do I say sorry?" she asked. She had one dimple on her left cheek that was visible even without a smile. I thought dimples came in pairs. She looked concerned, as if the question were genuine.

"You can," I said. "Cancer seems to confuse everyone."

"Are you sad?"

"Sure, I'm sad."

"Grammy has cancer. In her lungs," Ava said. "I don't feel sorry for her. But I think I feel sorry for your dad."

"Thanks."

"How come you haven't told Nina about your dad?" she asked.

"It hasn't come up."

"Are you embarrassed?"

"It's nothing to be embarrassed about."

FROM THE PARKING lot, Barker House of Corrections, with the dawn sky red and menacing behind it, looked pleasant. Sometimes I'd sit in my car and watch the other officers walk in finishing cigarettes, cursing, tucking in their shirts. The worst part of our day.

My phone rang. It was my father. I had seven minutes before punch-in.

"Three A.M. hits and what do you know, I'm up for the day," he said. It was the chemo.

"Reading puts me to sleep," I said.

"I can't read, too much on my mind. At work yet?"

I told him I was. I watched Officer Tully come out of the building and light a cigarette by the flagpole. He owed us a grand this week. He was betting Canadian football. All the guys had the itch. My dad and I were middlemen for a guy who ran a gambling website. My dad took the job after he retired from the post office. Some bookie from the old days, a big shot he'd run into again when he started spending his afternoons at the VFW Post on Carver Street, offered him 33 percent of losses. You can't say no to a cut like that. "A sweetheart deal for my former muscle," the bookie told him. My dad wouldn't tell me his name.

A long silence, as if he'd hung up or got cut off, then a snap of spit. I hated when he dipped on the phone.

"Good. Work is good. I think my body decided to kill me because I stopped working," he said. "Not something you want to hear but I'm going to say it. Your mother won't even let me say 'cancer.' She hears a radio ad for those cancer centers and she changes the station. I got no hair and a port in my chest but I can't say 'cancer.'"

When someone tells you they have cancer, or they're dying, you think back to the genesis. *Oh, he worked with asbestos in the sixties. Agent Orange, I bet that did it. She used to swim in that pond near the plant.* I did the guesswork with my dad. Stage four esophageal cancer. No surgery possible. Too embedded. I say it was beer and chewing tobacco. But he believed it was contaminated water from when he was stationed at Peterson Air Force Base. A friend of a friend at the VFW informed him of a class action lawsuit.

"She's worried, that's all," I said. I watched Tully and hoped my dad would let me go so I could catch him outside. Collecting was a hassle. The weekly visits were, too. I didn't need the money. With his pension and my mother still working, he didn't either. He wanted to go back in time, crack open the old ledger and probably some skulls.

Working the book with my dad gave him some happiness, and in his final months I couldn't take that away from him. He'd been a good father. A vet. A blue-collar worker, six days a week for thirty years. One wife. One home. Whatever inconvenience to me—the chase-downs, the hush-hush where people were locked up for doing what we were doing—I'd go along with. I had an obligation.

"I'm looking over last week's numbers. O'Brien," my dad said. "What's he doing betting women's tennis?"

"He's single, Dad. He's got Saturdays off."

"You're single and you don't bet tennis," he said. I heard him spit, then click his computer mouse more times than he should have. "Get him this week. Do I even need to say that? These Dana Farber trips. Boston and back at those hours. 'Be here for eight. You'll be out by two.' It's a friggin' shift. They should be paying *me*. Now that I'm pulled away sometimes I got to put more on you. Square up every week. That's how guys get in trouble. No matter how small, you get even before the next week begins."

"I'll get it all by Thursday," I said.

"Cancer! I have cancer!" he yelled into the phone. He coughed. "Don't worry, she's already off to work."

"Right," I said. "I'm going to catch up with someone. I'll see you Friday."

"We're up there in the black again. We keep it high enough you'll be all set," he said. "When I'm gone." He spat again.

"You're not going anywhere," I said.

———————

TULLY WAS A problem. He was much older than me—forty or so. He worked his ass off, twenty hours a week in overtime. He ran the Property Room, had the pleasure of conducting sixty strip-outs a day. It took a special type of officer to run Property. Off the tier, no partner, shut out in that room that smelled like someone shit in an old sock. Shriveled dicks and crusty brown-eyes all day. He had young kids, a couple of them; I didn't know their gender or age but you could tell the fathers from the bachelors. They put in early for holidays off, had Tupperware lunches, and raked in OT.

I found Tully alone in the locker room, standing at the sink. "Tough beat on the Alouettes," I told him.

"Got me on the wiggle," he said. His hair was messy. He wet it with sink water and combed it with his hands. He was thick, and I couldn't tell whether he was pudgy or muscular. Our uniforms could make you look great or terrible, no in-between. Whatever time of day it was, or night, Tully looked like he could fall asleep right there.

I could see he wanted to tell me about the loss. My father taught me, no matter how much you don't give a shit, to listen to a degenerate's bad beat. "What they want is to tell the story behind the loss," he'd said. "Losing is lonely."

"Thirty seconds to go and the kicker missed a chip shot," Tully said as he dried his hands on his pants.

"Shit," I said. It was quiet and I wondered if Tully even thought about owing me money, as if the loss was just some exercise and there wasn't a consequence. I was tired of chasing him down. I wanted him to go away. He was unimportant to me. He went to his locker and I went to mine. There were three slits in the top of my locker and that was where the officers slid in their envelopes. Inside were six of them. There was only one winner last week and I took two hundred out of an envelope to give to Hernandez on U7. I was usually discreet but I did it in the open, deliberately, so Tully would see me. He did but continued to shine his boots.

"You owe us a grand," I said.

He looked up, his face at ease; his hand gripped the shine brush. He said, "I can't swing it this week."

"You have to."

"I can't grow money, Piccard. I'll get it when I get it. What are you nagging me for?"

"Tomorrow," I said.

"Unlikely," he said, and kept looking at his boots.

"You don't bet what you can't pay."

I didn't give him time to say anything to that. I punched my locker, hard enough for effect. My dad would've told me to punch Tully, but I'd have to explain to my dad it wasn't the old days. I'd texted Tully his weekly numbers. He could rat. Plus, I couldn't hit him at the jail. I left the locker room not feeling better.

ANOTHER WEEK WENT by. I'd picked up Ava a couple more times from school. We went to McDonald's each time, and neither of us seemed to mind. I think she liked seeing me. And Tully was still avoiding me. I tried not to think about it but my father kept texting, *Where's your boy?* and *How'd you make out with your boy?* And then as I'd pulled in to work, another text: *Did you know county employee records are public?*

An inmate walked by me with her hair up in a bun held together by a pencil, and I told her to take it out. She did but looked at me like I'd called her ugly. It's against the rules, I told her.

The radio was busy that day. An officer on U9 made a medical emergency call and it took a few minutes before the lieutenant cleared it. Maybe a hanging, or some form of improvised suicide. But it was probably just a seizure, nothing to get excited about.

The unit feel was upbeat. It was Inmate Santoro's birthday and the girls made her a cake out of Ding Dongs, Ho Hos, and red M&M's. It was supposed to look like a baseball but looked more like a football, being brown and all. Santoro was a local celebrity. She'd gotten into it with a Yankees fan outside a bar and run him over. Sometimes at breakfast, I gave her an extra milk carton.

Nina came out and joined the girls when they cut the cake. She didn't look happy. I couldn't tell if it was an act. We hadn't been talking as much. I liked what I had with Ava, but the more I watched Nina from a distance, with a newer lens, I realized I knew nothing about her. There is winning a girl and then there is being fooled. I couldn't lose a job over the latter. If she was already taken, I needed to proceed with care. They sat around after singing "Happy Birthday" and watched a Kardashian yell at her husband on TV. I didn't have a piece. There wasn't enough to go around as it was.

When Nina went back into her cell I made a round and stood at the door. She told me to come in and when I did she kissed me. Her mouth was soft and I could taste the sugary cake. I stopped her before we could get going.

"We can't here," I said.

Nina sat on her bed. "I know. When I get out I'm giving you the best blow job of your life."

"You don't have to," I said. I remembered her ferocity during blow jobs, like my dick was a threat to her well-being and needed to be snuffed out. In a good way. It might not have been a great idea to accept one if I thought she wouldn't stick around for more. I didn't know if I was ready to bring one of the girls home, but Nina could be different. "Do you have a boyfriend?"

"You don't get to ask that."

"That's a bit unfair."

"I took a deal," she said. "Ninety days. The judge said if the jail lets me I could do work release. Maybe at the grocery store or something. You could bring Ava by to see me."

"I told you this case was nothing," I said. I couldn't tell if she was happy about the deal. "Ava is a good kid."

"She told me how great you are to her."

"I look forward to our little dates," I said, smiling. I meant that. Ava had given me a distraction from Tully, my dad, my empty apartment.

"Don't spoil her too much. I can't keep that up when I get home."

IT WAS THURSDAY, which was my work Friday. Lt. Hobson was reading the notes from the previous two shifts to the muster room full of officers. Tully wrote things down and looked attentive but wouldn't look my way. I hadn't told my dad that Tully had put me in a tough spot.

I flanked him in the west hallway as he was heading to Property. "Is this going to become a thing?" I asked.

"Listen, I have marital shit going on," he said. "I'm strapped. I messed up."

"Everyone has stuff going on. This is a thing now."

"What would Hobson think of your side business?" he asked.

"You would rat?" I said. "Think before you do. I'm not the only one in this place involved."

Tully dropped his hands. "Just give me time and you'll have nothing to worry about."

The next day, I drove up the steep street my parents lived on. From a few houses away I could see my dad in the backyard, his pale skin, the sheen on his bald head, standing on the side of the aboveground pool, leaning over the water, and holding the old, unwieldy pool vacuum handle. He was wearing brown wool winter gloves with no shirt. He'd opened the pool a few weeks ago, always the weekend after Memorial Day. But that summer it wouldn't get much use. His chemo treatment had a side effect where if he drank anything cold he'd feel like he was suffocating. Touching anything just below room temperature, like a metal spoon from a drawer, was like an electrocution. I didn't know what would happen if he fell into the pool. My mother was at work at the courthouse. They made her wear men's pants.

"Jesus, Dad," I said as I hopped the chain-link fence like I was twelve.

"Three bats in the filter already," he said, almost losing his balance. "Talk about a bad omen."

"Get down," I said and climbed the stairs of the deck. It was hot out. Behind my parents' house were thick wetlands bordered by high pine trees, giving the yard and half the pool some shade. But the heavy, humid air settled everywhere, immune to cover.

"Someone's got to do it," he said.

"I will. I brought my suit. If you fall in it'll be like sticking your dick in an outlet."

He looked up in agreement and laid the long vacuum stem on the side of the pool. I leaned off the deck and held my arm out and he shimmied off the side and onto the deck.

"Hand me a beer," he said. Six Bud Lights were lined up on the deck railing.

"One of these?" When I grabbed one it burnt me, and I realized why he'd put them there in the sunlight.

Still wearing the wool gloves, he drank a beer while I vacuumed the oval pool. He asked me how collection was going. I told him not to expect the grand from Tully but didn't tell him Tully might rat on us, ending the operation and maybe my career at the House.

"I warned you," he said. "This is coming out of your cut." He drank two more hot beers in silence. When he was ready to move on, he lectured me about sticking it out at the jail, about the security of a union and a pension. I could tell by his tone that he'd concluded I wasn't going to carry the ledger when he was gone. After only an hour my skin turned pink. I didn't mind sunburn. Working indoors, I wanted to look like it was summer.

We went inside and I made tuna sandwiches while he counted out the cash from the jail and added it to his pile. He huffed from his nostrils and tapped the bills. "What's this Tully guy's first name?"

"You can't do anything," I said and put his sandwich in front of him. "You'll get me jammed up at work."

"I'm not eating a grand. I'll just have a talk with him."

"Forget it. I'm not telling you his name. Take my cut. I don't need it."

"So what are we doing this for?"

I ate some tuna, then asked, "How's the treatment working?"

"Uncle John is taking me Monday for a PET scan," he said. He bit his sandwich. His head looked tiny without hair, his eyes threatening without eyebrows. I don't have his head. Mine looks normal shaved to the skin.

"Think there's any hope it shrunk?" I asked.

"Shit!" he yelled and dropped the pen he'd picked up to write in his ledger. "Shit, that is freezing."

"You have to be more careful. What if you fell in the water?"

He didn't answer. After he finished his sandwich he stood at the sink window and stared out at the pool. He sipped another beer. "Before this summer's over I'm going for one last swim."

I watched him squint out the window, then rub his head, where just last summer combable gray hair could be found.

———

TULLY'S TRUCK WAS parked outside his house, a colonial, with a red front door and moss on the roof. The windows had shutters and there was new white siding. A big oak tree stood tall and plumed over the dormer. A congenial home. A pink bike lay in the thick grass. I thought about Tully betting on Boise State, listening to the game on headphones while he cut his lawn.

"I knock, and when he answers, I'll grab him by the throat," my father said. He held his gloved hand open, all that was missing was a beer can.

"We agreed I go to the door, alone. It's the only way I do this." I was being insincere. He was going whether I'd gone along or not.

"Yes, sir."

I gave a long stare and then got out of my car. I crossed the dead-end street in the bright sun. The fealty of the dead end: no traffic, fixed neighbors, a fairly secure promise the road was forever tied off. The only other house looked quiet, with no cars. Middle of a workday, not many people would be home. But I knew it was Tully's day off. His kids would be at school, his wife at work.

I walked up the wooden steps and knocked loudly. A dog barked from the vacant house next door. It sounded big. I got a whiff of onions and looked around for the source. A terra-cotta pot to the left of the door, with long green blades sticking out straight, some topped with purple flowers. I bent and pinched off a blade. Chives. The door opened and I dropped the herb. Tully had on a white T-shirt and basketball shorts. His calves were thick and veiny.

"Are you fucking for real?"

"You put us in a bind," I said.

"Who's us?" he asked. "You show up on my day off to shake me down?"

"This isn't a shakedown. It's a friendly reminder."

"Bullshit. It's a shakedown," my father said from behind me.

"You brought your dad?"

"Some good faith, Tully. A couple hundred, anything," I said.

"I'm hard up. I've told you."

"Let's go inside," my dad said. "To talk."

I could feel my dad closing in behind me, right over my shoulder. He should've stayed in the car. Tully looked not scared but distracted, in a boyish way, like we'd interrupted him jerking off.

"We'll talk at work," said Tully, and he started to close the door. My dad rushed past me and drove the door open. He grabbed Tully by his shoulders and they fell into the house. It happened fast and I went inside without thinking and shut the door. Inside the house, the dog's bark was muffled. The two of them wrestled at the foot of a stairway. A laptop was open on the coffee table in the adjacent room, SportsCenter muted on the TV. Maybe he *had* been jerking it.

I'd seen my father fight a few times; the most memorable was when a customer on my newspaper route refused to pay overdue fees. Once I watched from my bedroom window as my father and his brother exchanged blows and fuck-yous in the driveway. I'd never seen him lose a fight and now he had my co-worker by the throat in his own home. Tully was squeaking out sounds, but no real words. My dad's feet were sliding on a rug. His shirt was pulled up, his tumor-ridden abdomen showing, and Tully, years younger and in better health, was unable to shake him.

"Even with cancer! You fucking seeing this, Mike?" my dad yelled, and he cocked back his right arm and punched Tully in his face.

Tully stopped struggling and, seemingly spent too, my father released his grip. Tully lay on his side, gasping. My father straddled him and gave a long, blank stare up toward the ceiling. I grabbed my father under the armpits and hoisted him until he was standing.

"I don't have it," Tully said. He spat blood into his hand. "Do what you want, I just don't have it."

There was nothing more to do, short of us robbing the house, so I told my dad it was time to go. He walked slowly behind me across the street, victorious, taking in the scenery. He got inside the car and clapped his hands loudly.

"Yes," he said.

I started driving away. "Yes, what? You know what you just did? I'm fucked at the House. You just made life hell for me."

My father held his palm out and I looked away from the road to see a gold wedding band sitting on the glove.

"That's probably worth like a hundred bucks," I said.

"That's not the point, Mike. Not the point at all."

———————————

"ARE YOU GOING to bring me to McDonald's every time?" Ava asked. She'd lost her second canine tooth on the bottom. It was strange to see up close, the loss and growth of teeth. I'd forgotten the process.

"I don't know where else to take you."

"I'm sick of eating these. I don't really even like them."

"Why didn't you say something?"

"I was trying to be nice."

We sat while I tried to think of something else. She had on that girls-and-monsters shirt again. The same pink shorts with the ink stains. I wondered if Nina told Ava about the plea deal, or if Ava told Nina about my dad and my urinal issues. Maybe

I was only a means to keep them connected. I didn't know what I was to anyone.

"How is your dad doing?"

"I don't know," I said. "We haven't spoken in a few days."

"Why not?"

"It's complicated."

"I'm not stupid."

"I know that. You might be the smartest person I know."

She smiled. "Can we see a movie?"

"I don't think so. It'll be late. Wouldn't your Grammy be worried?"

"She doesn't even hear me come in."

"Too tired from work?"

"I've never seen her have a job."

Nina had lied. I was beginning to question why I had any interest in her. If I dropped my enthusiasm for Nina, where would that leave Ava and me? This could be the last time I saw her. "I'm not a big movie person."

"Do you have a pool?" she asked.

"My apartment complex has one but I've never seen it open."

She slid the cup of melting ice cream to the center of the table. She was disappointed. "I'm not allowed back in the one at our apartment."

"What'd you do?"

"People make things up," she said.

"Did they post a photo of you? Who cares? Go back."

"There's only two lifeguards. Trust me—they remember me."

"Maybe I can talk to them."

"Please don't bring me home yet," she said. "I don't want to go home."

I couldn't imagine not wanting to go home as a kid. She stared at the table. If she was playing me, she didn't have to work so hard.

"If I go in that stupid ball pit, will you come with me?" I asked.

We were the only ones in the pit and we whipped the light balls at each other. She dove in and grabbed at my ankles and tried pulling me under. She said something from inside the balls, *cunt* maybe, but I couldn't be sure. We laughed and I gave her ten fingers a few times so she could do a full flip into the pit. The people who watched from the restaurant weren't laughing with us but they should have been. I hadn't laughed for real in a long time. My phone vibrated in my shorts pocket so I held my hands up to Ava in surrender. She let one last ball fly by my head while I checked my phone. It was my dad. I had to answer. "Are you okay?"

"Eighty dollars," he said.

"What?" I asked.

"That's what I got for his ring. Come get your take, whenever." He hung up the phone.

"What is it?" Ava asked.

"Still want to go for that swim?"

It was hot inside the car, the sun beating on the leather seats and steering wheel. We stood outside with the doors open to air it out. In the middle of the busy street, seagulls yelled at each other and fought over spilled french fries and a white bag. Cars drove around them and a city bus beeped its loud horn and they flew off.

We drove to my parents' and I let Ava sit in the front seat. She messed with the radio and tapped her bare knees. I thought about my dad, what he'd done to Tully. In all the excitement, I never asked how his PET scan went.

When we pulled up, Ava said, "I don't have a bathing suit." I shouldn't have dragged her there. My dad would ask about her. But he'd liked Nina back in high school. He'd be happy we reconnected.

"You can wear a big T-shirt."

My mother was at work again. She'd be fine, I knew, with keeping herself busy. We went through the front door and I told Ava to wait in the living room while I got her one of my dad's old green shirts with the big shamrock on the front. When I came back, she was holding a photo of me as a kid.

"This is a really nice house," she said.

I'd never heard anyone call the house nice. I handed her the shirt. She thanked me and I showed her where the bathroom was. I went back to the kitchen to see if my dad was outside. He was in his bathing suit standing at the edge of the deck, facing the pool. He put his thin arms out and dove into the water. He came up out of the water and flailed his arms in the air, and then he gave a loud shriek.

Out the window I yelled, "Get out of the water!"

He directed his head toward the sound of my voice but his eyes were somewhere else. He didn't answer me. Ava hurried up next to me in the green shirt. She had tied her hair up with one of my mother's hair ties. My dad shook and rocked and splashed water with his fists like he was fighting it.

"If the water is that cold I do not want to go in," Ava said.

"It's not," I said. "I'll explain it all later."

It was not until I was dragging my father out of the pool, with Ava reaching down, grabbing at his biceps, trying to help, that I realized she'd never forget this. It'd stay with her forever and it wouldn't be up to her.

H er mother used to restore old dolls, specifically, American compo dolls. Madame Alexander, Amberg. One of her last memories of her mother, it must have been a Sunday afternoon, when she would invite Brenner to stand at the sink with her and watch her take the green out of a doll's mohair wig. It was such a careful process. The doll would be covered in plastic wrap so it wouldn't get wet. Each strand of hair was massaged in the soapy water, then brushed with a metal comb. She'd fill cracks, airbrush their faces, paint their eyes and mouths, so gentle, and her strokes clean, but then she'd scuff them. "No one wants a doll that looks new," she'd say. The dolls were sent to her in the mail. She cared for them as if they were the owners' children. Brenner was tempted to play with the dolls, but it was her mother's work, and she wouldn't have dared. In this last memory, maybe the last before breast cancer took her, her mother made up a doll's face, with charcoal eyebrows and magenta cheeks, and though Brenner couldn't remember her mother's face much from that day, that doll's face remained with her.

Inside the Property Room, Brenner stood before a clown-faced junkie, pupils pointed down, thick red lipstick cracked and smeared, still groggy from whatever she'd swallowed or stuck in her arm before her arrest. The woman was young, younger than Brenner, who was twenty-five. Hobson called her a whippersnapper, and she didn't think he knew what it meant. He might as well pat her head and give her a sticker. Nashua had scooped up six women in a prostitution ring, and Brenner was sure to spend her entire break searching holes for bags.

"Fishhook your cheeks," Brenner explained, miming the action. "Straighten up. I said straighten up. With your fingers. Fishhook."

The new admit was nude, her skin bruised in all sorts of places, but the ones that stood out to Brenner were the deep blue ones on her armpits. She stumbled and caught herself against the bricked wall, then leaned there. Behind her were shelves of bagged and boxed inmate property, shoes, jewelry, clothes, suits dropped off by loved ones or good lawyers for court. The large closet-like room smelled like wet sneakers. Behind Brenner was a shower where inmates rinsed, like at a public pool. They'd dry off and get walked through the unclothed search procedure. Other than the Bubble on Max, which was a boys' club for male officers to pack dips and nap, the Property Room was the only room that was not under video surveillance.

"Hon, you need to get this over with," Brenner said. Brenner took the few steps that were in between them and she helped the woman stand up. "I'm going to inspect your mouth. Then I'm going to bend you over at the waist and check you. Can you do this with me?"

The inmate nodded, her dry tongue peaked between her crusted lips. Brenner checked her mouth. She'd been working at the jail for a year and she had learned much about people. How bad people's teeth could get. The inmates—the hookers and women with gangrene arms—their teeth could get rocklike, gravelly. Dr. McKiel, the county dentist, didn't get paid nearly enough.

The inmate's breath smelled like cigarettes. Brenner grabbed her around the waist with her left arm and pushed her into a bow with her other hand. The inmate let all her weight collapse in Brenner's grasp and her arms hung limp. Brenner struggled to hold her up and spread her feet to get a stronger stance, then inspected the inmate's vagina and anus as respectfully as one could.

Hunter retired, so Brenner was the only female officer on first shift. Radio calls all day: "Brenner, 10-11 Property." As a policy, men couldn't change out the women. Strip searches gave her an affinity for the inmates. She didn't like that. She wanted to be hard on them. But if one was in distress, or agitated, the male officers would call her down to U1 or Booking, and she'd be expected to calm them. The male officers were never expected to calm anyone. They'd move right past verbal de-escalation and straight to force. With this approach, voice before fists, they could mistake Brenner's professionalism for sympathy. The men called her an inmate hugger. And she could be guilty of sympathizing with them. Some were pregnant, or thought they might be, or missed the children they had. But sympathy inside the House was a weakness, and that made her think of her father. He was fascinated by her decision to work at the House. "You're obviously trying to prove something," he'd said, working over his eggs and Tabasco, "but they're going to eat you alive." Did he say that? It felt like something he'd say. No one had eaten her alive. She'd look in the mirror before muster each morning and say "Fuck you." Best softball pitcher in Merrimack Valley history. Dominated in D1. Graduated summa cum laude in criminal justice. Signed on at Securitas and patrolled the old mills now turned apartments. Bided her time for a real law enforcement job. Where did he expect her to work? It was always going to be a badge.

Outside the Property Room, Tully took over and escorted the inmate to the large holding tank. Tully, the Property officer, was stocky, prominent brow with black hair combed to the right. He lent Brenner his leather gloves when she had to dig into pockets; would sometimes tell her, when an inmate seemed strange or agitated or drunk, "I'll be right outside this door if you need me." She never did need him, or the coddling aspect of the male/female officer relationship. Or the other way, the male officers who raised their voices, yelled, postured, and pushed her aside. It took her most of her first year to figure out how to be. She requested a bigger, baggier uniform. She stopped smiling and saying thank you to officers who held doors for her, wrote more D-tickets for violations of 3.1 of the inmate handbook, Disrespect to Officer. As much as she wanted to get a drink after work, she didn't join the first shifters at Willie's.

Tully was married, and she looked forward to their interactions each day. They shared a sick-humored small talk that bordered on flirtation. He'd ask her how the fish market was today. She'd tell him clammy. He'd laugh and spit cherry Skoal juice in his cup, tell her the girls in the tank asked if she was single. "You be the judge. If they're cute . . ." she'd say. He looked forward to seeing her too, she knew, because he perked up whenever she came into Property. Tully was an abrasive officer, the kind that treated the job as a sentenced penalty, so far removed from the excitement of the early days, and now every task was a trial, every inmate an enemy.

When Tully returned to the Property Room, Brenner was digging through a trash bag, attempting to fulfill a request from an inmate on U9, who wanted his court clothes released to his mother for dry cleaning, a common request.

"You're a perfect soft-ass with the inmates," he said. "Giving out hugs for all."

"I was sick of looking at her scabs."

"You doing my job now?" Tully asked and picked up the inmate request form off the counter.

"I can't find the forty-five hundreds. You'd think they'd be right after the forty-fours."

"It's like some shitbag taught you how to work the room," he said.

He'd shown her the CCN groupings, the specific bags that held certain items: black bags for suits and coats, boxes for shoes and jewelry, trash bags for any other clothing. She felt the system to be crude, mainly the trash bags, but it worked for Tully and there was no reason for him to change it. After a few days, he'd begun to quiz her. He'd call out a CCN and she'd walk to the grouping, find the bag or box, and pull out the item requested. She was excited how easily she picked it up. Though it was not difficult, she didn't want to look stupid in front of Tully, nor show him up by making it look too easy. She would play dumb, mistakenly grab the wrong bag, or ask him for a hint. But once, he patted her back and she moved away. She paused. He had already moved on to another bag but she could still feel his hand on her back and she couldn't help but think of her father. Intention. She watched him move about the room deliberately.

And now she was searching in the wrong spot. She only had one strip-out, and she wanted to linger a bit, to not leave and return to her unit. "Can you help me?"

"You don't need to do this anyways," he said. "But I'll help. You're six or seven feet in the wrong direction."

Tully walked behind her and went down the line of bags and pointed to where she should have been. "Here," he said. "Since you insist, I'm going to get lunch."

After he left, Brenner wanted to call him back—for what, she didn't know. She abandoned the search for the right bag and left the Property Room to return to her unit. She walked down the west hallway toward the elevators outside Central

Control and listened to the chatter on the radio, officers calling for doors to be opened, Lt. Hobson putting out a call for overtime takers to no response, it being a Saturday. She stayed close to the wall and walked upright, knowing she was being watched by the two officers in Central, most likely making comments about her demeanor or if they would bang her. The male officers were judged by their size: the big ones were dumb; the skinny ones were pussies. Pigs.

She took the elevator alone, then walked down the second-floor east hallway, through the sliding doors, and then she entered U4's sally port, a small enclosure surrounded by windows, one magnetized locking door to get in the unit and another to leave. The exit door secured behind her. Through the windows, she could see Menser idling on the mezzanine, watching the inmates lift weights. The inner door wouldn't unlock until he strolled down to the control panel and let her in. But the door had some give so she ripped at the handle, enough to force the magnet to bang it back shut. Nothing from Menser. An inmate sat inside the door at the first dayroom table and watched her. He had a hairy mole on his chin, tattooed neck, bedhead. She banged the door again. Menser noticed her but wasn't budging. She returned Mole Face's stare and, in the air, drew a 3 1. He rubbed his groin. The minute she got on the floor, she thought, Mole Face was getting locked in. But her eyes combed the dayroom and she saw many more men staring. And now she was stuck in the sally port, smothered by the weight of all the stares of men she didn't know but disliked. Couldn't write them all up. And it triggered a feeling inside, like she was a model for them, an animated magazine cutout. She's seen their jerk-off material: Victoria's Secret catalogs, photos from chubby girlfriends, escort ads from the phone book, newspaper clippings. They could get off to anything, and they did, and they were staring to pack away her body for later. Recently, when she left the Property Room, she had stood outside the door and put her ear to it. After only a few seconds, she heard Tully turn the radio on, listen to sports talk. She could hear long zippers and then boxes tumble, like he was rushing.

END OF OCTOBER. A month of Brenner's visits to Property. It was yet another New England fall that could be mistaken for winter, the air damp and cold. Tully had become less talkative. Brenner felt she'd become uninteresting and decided to tell him about her curb shopping. When driving through Nashua and Hudson, she would pull her RAV4 over when she noticed furniture left on someone's curb that looked like something she could work with: armoires, desks, dressers, pub tables, and stools and chairs, whatever was small enough to cram into the trunk. At home after her shifts, she would undress, change into an old T-shirt and jeans, go into the second bedroom, and continue working on whatever piece of furniture she had started on. The room smelled of wood and paint. The carpeted floor was covered with a tan canvas drop cloth, spattered with a year's worth of work. Her joy was in the sanding and painting and staining, she told him; repurposing something someone else no longer had any use for, then furnishing her apartment with it. Her coffee table was an antique chest. The two side tables next to her couch were wooden chicken crates. The bookshelf in her bedroom was three coffee tables stacked on each other, stained chestnut. She didn't tell Tully about her mother's dolls, how sometimes she asked her dead mother if the finished product looked all right.

They searched bags and laid out the day's court transit attire. It was early, and every so often Tully sipped from his coffee cup. He closed his eyes before each sip, like he was afraid of the coffee's heat. He didn't say anything about her hobby. His pleated pants were tight on his thighs. He hadn't shaved in days.

In the way of Tully's happiness seemed to be his marriage, but he would never say. It could be as simple as falling out of love with his wife, trying to keep her happy in the aftermath. Or maybe he never loved his wife.

She looked over her shoulder and watched him. She liked the way he looked, with his arms at his side boyishly, smiling, his hair loose from the part and curled down his forehead. She wondered how she looked to him, if he wished her black hair to be down. And then he turned to her and looked at her as so many of the inmates did, with an intent gaze, as if she were not his equal, as if the inmates were not inferior, and she wanted to leave.

"What is it?" she asked.

"Nothing." He held his stare.

"Don't make this something."

"You started it," he said, and moved back to the bags.

She had her reasons for not wanting to get involved with Tully. For one thing: he'd stop being a real man. There is no worse person than a man with impudence, who's received what he's been aching for. She remembered Dylan from high school, his bony body, his weed-smelling hair, his disregard for the power she had given him. She slept with him on Saturday and Sunday of that weekend in a tiny beach cottage, and his proud casualness made her want the weekend to be over, to forget his spit, the taste of cinnamon liquor, the laughter outside the bedroom door. Dylan disappointed her, not in the usual first-time disappointment. She was new and he was seasoned, had a method during sex that was practiced. And he was rough and adamant on coming on her breasts, her neck, and laughed as he came, then bragged afterward. She could still feel him on her skin days later, the smell of come chemical-like and hazardous like paint thinner.

She needed to change the subject. "I once found a gun rack, more like a cabinet. It had a glass window in the door and the glass was spidered with a hole the size of a fist," she said.

He pulled down a box and slid it across the brown-and-white-checkered floor toward her feet.

"Farquhar is requesting his silver wedding band," he said. "It should be in there."

Brenner opened the box and began rummaging through the items: a rough-bristled comb, a gold chain, a leather wallet torn on the seam, held together by a safety pin.

"It's funny. No, it isn't. I mean it's funny that you fix stuff up. Trash. I've imagined what you do outside of here but I'd never imagined that."

She kept looking in the box but stopped searching for the ring.

"I mud wrestle in bars," she said. "I'm a shopaholic. I go to movies alone, but I buy two tickets so the teller doesn't think I'm weird."

"Not like that," he said. "I imagine you making coffee in the morning. What TV shows you watch at night. If we're watching the same thing." He unzipped a black property bag, then stood still in front of it.

"I could be guilty of thinking about you."

"All the time?" he asked.

She bent back down and ran her hands through the box. She heard him walk toward her and she kept her back to him. Though she was pretty certain he was going to kiss her, it might still be a gag, and when she turned he would be wearing underwear on his head. But he put his hand on her shoulder and she stood up and he turned her and he kissed her. The turn was forceful, as was the stubble on his chin against her chin. He kept on her like he wanted to get the most out of the kiss before she pushed him off. But she did not push him. She held her eyes shut and he turned his chin over and continued the kiss on the other side of her mouth. His aftershave and deodorant were fragrant, both a cool spicy wintergreen. When she felt his chest against hers, then his excitement against her, she pulled away. He pulled her back and kissed her again and his hand went to her breast, then to her neck. His hands were strong. They un-tucked each other's shirts and Brenner started to unbutton Tully's shirt. He pulled himself out and she touched him and he put his hand down her pants and touched her.

"No," she said, turning her face.

He kept rubbing her, kissing her neck.

"Tully, stop. Please."

"I know. I know."

He turned from her and fixed his uniform.

He said, "I've never done this before."

Brenner didn't want to allow him the satisfaction. If she was his first cheat, she'd been given a reverence unworthy of anyone before.

But it was disgraceful, and Brenner didn't feel that until she left the Property Room, the controlled air in the hallway dry and fake, the lighting in the ceiling bright, all of it produced. She wanted to leave the building and stand outside and breathe.

Back in her unit Menser seemed annoyed at the length of her absence, all intentional huffs and groans. She feared she smelled like Tully, it clung to her, her sense of smell heightened by aware-ness, like when she hid her cigarettes from her father. But Menser didn't look back at her, just bent into the control panel, opened the inner door 4018A, and let himself off the unit for lunch.

———

THE TOOTHLESS PROSTITUTE stood before her in a ragged pink Juicy Couture shirt, silver-jeweled, ripped Juicy jeans, and high winter boots.

"Show me your hands. Good. Wiggle your fingers. Now run them through your hair. Mouth. What's that?"

"A tongue ring."

Brenner had grown tired of the searches, the monotony of ceremony, the stripping down of another woman to nothing. She could make them feel violated inside the inelegant Property Room, calling to order their wrongdoings. There, in their nakedness, Brenner could make them feel any number of ways. Because of this, she may have dreaded the searches more than the inmates.

"You need to remove the ring," Brenner said and held out her gloved hand.

The new admit fumbled with the rod but got it out. After she placed it on Brenner's hand, a string of saliva hung from the inmate's fingers to Brenner's. The inmate shook her hand, disconnecting the two of them, and wiped the saliva on her leg.

After dismissing the inmate, sending her back to the tank in Booking to await her transport, Brenner waited in the Property Room for Tully.

He came in and quickly looked away from her. She looked past him at the rows of black bags, the cubbies underneath with boxes of wedding rings and keepsakes, black trash bags of dirty clothes last worn by people losing their freedom.

———————————

THE FIRST WEEK in November, Menser's mother died. Brenner had worked with him for a few months and it was the custom anyway to attend any wakes regardless of how well you knew another officer. The day of, she put on a dress she hadn't worn in a long time, not since starting at the jail, and she straightened her naturally curly hair.

But she rushed through the funeral home and the wake, suddenly aware that seeing Tully and his wife was a possibility. Her brevity disconcerted her. Tully had made her feel wrong and not herself. And now, on her short drive home through Nashua, she decided she wouldn't allow Tully to make her feel that way.

The late afternoon sun glinted off the cars parked along the sides of roads, lined with houses packed so close they lacked driveways. Brenner glanced at curbside freebies: a lawn mower, a toy kitchen, a mattress leaned against a chain-link fence. At a red light, she noticed a bench with a cracked laundry basket on top filled with paint cans. On the next block she pulled over, and in her black dress and heels, she walked back down the street toward the bench. The wind blew heavily, leaves loose and free twisted past her. She'd forgotten her jacket in the crossover. The traffic at the light was stopped and she tried not to think about the people watching her, their comments or quips to other passengers. She placed the laundry basket on the sidewalk. It was a Santa Fe–style bench but that didn't matter because she was taking it anyway. She dragged it, walking backward, feeling the vibration of pine on cement. When she reached the trunk of her crossover, as if in her sweatpants and T-shirt, she heaved the bench clumsily inside.

WHEN BRENNER WORKED on pieces she'd picked up, she took her time. She sanded off the name ABIGAIL in red paint from the yellow pine children's bench. She could have stopped when the lettering was faint. But with her face mask and work glasses on she drove her shoulder and wrist into the bench along the grain, the bottom of the *g* giving her the most resistance, each stroke taking off more layers, deeper into wood, away from what it was and who it had been for.

When she was done sanding and stripping it, the bench now a blank canvas, she decided to paint it a bright red and keep it nameless. It took her two hours for the first coat. While it dried, with a dust mask hanging from her ears, she sat at her computer table, a Chatelet writing desk she'd bought at an estate sale in Salem for eleven dollars. She ran her fingers over the wood. She could make money doing this. She looked over her accent chest, its curved legs, its ginkgo-leaf pulls, the care she'd taken with it. The Biedermeier armchair. The maple dough box end table. That took her most of February. But what kind of career was that? Releasing something you worked so hard on? Carrying Officer Kelley on her back up six flights of stairs during the academy, not quitting, not crying, though she'd wanted to, meant something. Her swollen thighs after hundreds of prisoner squats. Being pepper-sprayed in the showers. Captain Dixon's face when he pinned the badge on her chest, how she knew he never thought she'd be beside him on the podium.

She searched Facebook for Joe Tully, and on his profile page she clicked on *Married to Kathy Gaudette-Tully.* Tully's wife had a chubby face, brown hair, a profile picture that cropped her out from the neck down.

The next night, the bench with two proper coats on and dried, was again stuck into the back of the crossover. Brenner drove toward 10 Hanover Road, easily found on BeenVerified, a website she hadn't known existed. Hanover, a dead-end turnoff from Miles Road, a long road that went all the way back into Massachusetts and north right up to the jail. Brenner found the house and drove past it, spun around the cul-de-sac, looked for any signs of outdoor activity, but it was cold and dark and Tully was probably putting his kids to bed or helping with homework, fumbling over math problems or reading vocabulary sentences. Or maybe the kids were really young, she didn't even know, and Tully was making love to Kathy while thinking about Brenner. Tully could just be doing dishes, or watching TV with his feet up, biting his fingernails because he couldn't dip in front of the kids. Or maybe Tully was the kind of father who *could* dip in front of the kids. A master of his home. Whatever it was he was doing inside the white colonial, with the left side of the house lit up from the inside, Brenner didn't want to focus on it.

She pulled along the front lawn, which was lined with a dozen filled leaf bags. The lawn was well kept and evenly cut, the moon in the clear night sky showing off Tully's husbandry in the dark. Brenner was a hiccup, a reprieve from Tully's domestic indigestion. She felt again a girl, learning sex with Dylan, embarrassed and anxious to grow to a time when it was all easy. With the car running, she got out and pulled the bench from the trunk, dragged it slowly so as not to make a sound, and abandoned it in the center of Tully's lawn.

BRENNER KEPT HER distance from Tully for the next couple of weeks. It was difficult. She still saw him every day during her shift but she did the strip search and then left the Property Room and went back to her unit. He did not prod her or hang around the room when she left. Though some days she hoped for it, she'd come out into the Booking hallway and he wouldn't be right outside the door.

Then in December, Lt. Hobson approached her before a shift and asked her if she could re-acclimate Officer Tully to unit work.

"I noticed he taught you the Property Room," Hobson said.

Brenner must've looked odd because Hobson said, "You signed off on some property request forms."

"Sure," she said. "No problem, sir."

On the unit, Brenner took the lead. She took the radio, did the head count, and wrote out the opening log. Tully walked around the unit, peered into the showers, fiddled with a pair of nail clippers that had been broken for some time. He ignored Brenner. He was quiet, nodded to her at times, refused to make eye contact. He alphabetized the inmate ID tags. He channel-flipped for groups of indecisive TV watchers. Outside the Property Room and exposed on the unit, he looked new and unsure, like a freshly booked inmate.

The unit was easy enough to run by herself. It wasn't like there were heavy bangers up on U4. And she had also been there for six months, knew every inch of the triangular, two-tiered unit. She could rattle off all of the sixty-eight inmate bunk assignments from memory, started to even remember laundry bag numbers, surprised herself when things she hadn't tried to memorize began to pop into her head when needed. "Inmate Hanes? Bottom bunk, cell 17. Bad back. Upper bunk restriction. I believe he's in the shower."

She didn't come out and ask about the move and also didn't hear anything in the rumor mill. She watched him mosey around, avoid confrontation, stick only to friendly inmate interactions, lean against the wall where she wondered if he'd fallen asleep.

At lunch she asked Officer O'Brien what was going on with Tully's move. O'Brien didn't question her interest and told her, rather hushed over his black coffee, that Tully's marriage had proceeded to an ugly divorce. He'd recently gotten his third DUI, maybe a week or so ago. If O'Brien had to guess, one DUI was a mistake, the second a tragic oversight, the third a career killer. She wanted to un-hear the news. She didn't see Tully as a drinker. She couldn't really imagine what he was. She knew as much about him as she did about the inmates on the tier.

AT LEAST MENSER wouldn't put up with catcalls. The staring he didn't mind. But something about the inmates' yells and whistles made him red. It was as easy a D-ticket as they come, easy even for him, and they all had to make the monthly quota Hobson had laid down. Brenner kept her 3.1 D-tickets colorful, made sure to get the exact wording. *Bitch gives me porn dick.* Tully was so checked out, he didn't write any tickets, and it was hard for Brenner to write up each infraction. But there were more important tasks than a handful of tickets: running the entire unit, chow, cleaning details, nurse call, programs, pat-downs, cell searches. It was starting to be too much for her to handle alone. She would normally call out each asshole, knowing if she let one get away with it, she'd be back to the beginning, back to her blossoming days, back to hiding herself from the eyes of gas pumpers and grocery baggers and her friends' fathers.

After making a routine round, poking her head into a few cells, she gloved up and approached Tully and told him she needed assistance searching 2327. He followed her up the metal stairs. The unit was active with dominoes and TV, showers and phones. Inside the cell, they began searching, left to right, top to bottom.

"I'm losing control of the unit," she said as she flipped through sheets of paper from the desk cubby. "I need a partner."

"There's nothing in this cell but crispy socks," he said.

"I'm not playing around." She stopped searching. "What, this is punishment?"

"What did you do that was wrong?"

Brenner left Tully in the cell. She de-gloved, walked the tier, and it was like she couldn't hear anything at all.

THE NEXT MORNING, she ironed one of her older, tighter uniform shirts. She put on a light coat of blush, some eyeliner. In muster, she kept her head down, hoping Hobson wouldn't call her out. No makeup. No piercings. Jail bun, that's all. She walked down to the unit with Tully next to her and he didn't say anything. They hadn't spoken about what happened in the Property Room since it happened. The silence between them had gone on so long that it was comforting and speaking to each other would be painful. But in this short walk down the east hallway, alone, she could break the silence. If she didn't then, they'd be on the unit, in front of the inmates, and it'd be another day she'd ... She stopped him with her arm.

"I'm sorry about everything happening to you," she said.

Tully took a deep breath. "It's happening because of me."

They were standing outside the unit outer door. The hallway was quiet; the artificial lighting above them faint; the walls bricked and bare.

"I'm not going to tell you what to do," she said. "But it can't be good for you to keep this up."

He looked around but not at her, like he was anxious. "What about you? What are you doing?" he asked. "You're embarrassing yourself."

He turned and pushed the door open into the sally port. She followed him.

After head count, with the doors unsecured, she made her rounds. Inside an empty cell, she dropped her hair down into a ponytail. The inmates let her pass carefully; she didn't need to turn around to know they turned themselves to watch her walk on. A few seemed unsure. Some of the older ones gave her disapproving looks from their tables. Back at the officer station from her round she saw Tully watching her, crossing and uncrossing his arms with an uncomfortable shifting of shoulders on the wall, couldn't find a good side to sleep on.

During noon lockdown and head count, she told Tully to go to lunch break first. They switched off, as all partners on the units did, and she'd gone first the day before. She sat at a table, and instead of going on break, Tully came over and sat with her.

The unit was quiet except for some toilets flushing, then an occasional laugh from a cell. They were sitting at the table in front of the officer station. The unit smelled terrible after lunch, all the inmates going back to their cells to relieve the food they claimed was laced with laxatives. Tully sat across from her and he laid his hands out on the table.

"I wouldn't take back what I did," he said.

She nodded.

He looked away and watched the clock on the far wall. His sadness was enough to make her afraid for him. She couldn't understand the way he let his face get, close to collapsing into a sob. The silence of the unit was everywhere around them but not between them. She wasn't against him. If they weren't on the unit, in a place anywhere but where they were, she'd put her hand out. She imagined doing it, she imagined him putting his hand on hers but never looking at her, never acknowledging it.

His chin was tucked into his clip-on tie. He still wouldn't look back at her. She wanted to be back in the Property Room.

"Did you happen to see Wilkerson fall coming down the stairs?" she asked.

He laughed, seemed happy to change the subject. "I did. Poor bastard's leg keeps getting worse."

"It's like his leg stutters."

He laughed again and this time looked at her. His mouth finally looked natural again, lips spread out, cheeks heightening. His eyes were squinted and raw, like he'd been in a dark room and someone turned a light on him.

"Maybe he's running out of batteries," he said.

She checked her watch.

"You left that bench on my grass," he said. "My daughter thinks it was the tooth fairy. She's got it up in her room."

"The tooth fairy has it too easy. No work and all the credit."

"You should go to break. Wash up."

"I'm not done yet."

Head count cleared over the intercom and they both stood and walked to the officer station. The inmates opened their doors, came out, sat at dayroom tables for TV watching, some pulled off their shirts and started pulling at the weights, others circled the officer station and control panel, eyeing the partners.

Brenner unrolled the control panel cover by slowly bending at her waist, grasped the long silver handle with a deliberately tender grip, looked up and smiled toward a group of inmates sitting at a table. A sitcom played on the TV behind her.

Inmate Robinson, under his breath but certainly loud enough for her to hear, said, "I want a bite of that."

Brenner straightened and looked at Tully. He walked out from behind the control panel and stood in front of Robinson, who was sitting on a stool where Tully had just been sitting.

"A bite of what?" Tully asked.

"I didn't say nothin.'"

"Too pussy to say it again?"

Robinson pretended to watch the TV. Brenner knew where this ended and she wasn't about to stop it. She saw a life in Tully. She wanted him to have this moment.

"That's what I thought. Lock in, *in*mate," Tully said.

Robinson shook his head. "It wasn't me."

"You have two seconds. Lock the fuck in."

Robinson sat tilted on the stool, leaning on his elbow on the table. Inmates were hanging over the railing on the top tier; some had come halfway down the stairs. Tully pointed up to the crowd, told them to get the fuck off the stairs. He had his hands out in front of him, his sleeves tight around his biceps, his chest squared on Robinson. Brenner stood still, her hand over the radio mic clipped on her shoulder. She knew Robinson was going to cower to Tully. She knew she wouldn't need to make a call. But she didn't want to seem like a bystander.

Robinson slowly got up and walked up the stairs and stood in the threshold of his cell, 13. Tully walked backward to behind the panel, unrolled the cover without looking away from Robinson, and released cell 13 from its lock. Robinson closed the door in front of him slowly. Tully turned to Brenner and winked at her convincingly like he would have in the safety of his Property Room. He rolled the cover back up and made a round with long strides, the inmates letting him pass with enough space for two of him.

T he day after Sam Knudsen shot himself, we gathered at the tap house we frequented on occasions like retirements, birthdays, anniversaries, and once, a send-off party when Connelly left for his second tour, but never returned.

O'Brien was drunk when he walked in, having had the day off. He joined the four of us. We sat there at three in the afternoon after shift and we drank deconstructed Irish car bombs in our white undershirts; all of us except O'Brien were still wearing our brown county-issued slacks and boots. Someone in the bar played a dozen straight Guns N' Roses songs and I spent most of the next hour searching the other patrons, trying to figure out which asshole would do such a thing. O'Brien recommended we get cross-eyed and tell stories about Sam Knudsen. He said that's how the Irish mourned. We were fine with it. Greenly drank two beers and two Bushmills to everyone else's one. He kept asking why Sam Knudsen would kill himself with a bullet to the head. His wife wouldn't be able to have an open casket at the wake. The more Greenly drank the more we could feel the desperation in his voice. *How could he?* didn't feel like a rhetorical question but one in which Greenly yearned for an answer only Sam could give. Cartel didn't say anything at all.

After we were all feeling pretty wet, Cartel warmed up. He spun a half-full shot glass in between his forefinger and thumb and told a story about the day he and Sam Knudsen floored a monster of an inmate on U6. He said he'd never gone for the guy with only one other officer but this time he had Knudsen. He didn't tear up, his voice didn't crack. Nothing like that. He just talked to the shot glass and we drank and listened and no one interrupted him or asked questions.

Greenly told us about the day his father died. How Greenly had been cutting the lawn when his wife ran out to him with the news and he'd only got it half done, the uncut portion noticeably longer. He stood there wondering what to do. His father couldn't use his help; he was gone. The bastard had remarried and ran off to Florida anyway. His wife cried in his arms. It was an otherwise beautiful day. Sun, birds—that kind of shit. Greenly struggled with how wrong it'd look if he sent her inside and finished the lawn. He decided to walk into the house with her and calm her down and when she was good he went back out and finished. We all agreed he wasn't wrong in doing that. I wanted to tell them about my father and how he died. But it was recent and from painful cancer and there really wasn't a point to attempting to describe it.

Cartel got real talkative. He told us about a time, when he was fifteen, he'd found a cat wandering around his house and he took it in. The cat was fine for a few months and his father told him he'd need to care for it or it was gone. It started pulling up pieces of the carpet in the living room and then one day Cartel came home from school and the cushion to the couch was spilled out all over the room. He tried to get all the stuffing back in before his dad came home and his mother even helped him. The pieces were too small, too much of them, and his father walked into the mess and ordered Cartel to take care of the cat. Cartel wrapped the cat in a sheet and brought it out into the yard and dug a hole. He tossed the sheet into the hole and he shot the cat with his hunting rifle. Cartel told us the cat was a fighter. It didn't die right away. It actually got one paw ripped through the sheet before it stopped moving.

O'Brien asked why the hell Cartel would tell that story. He looked to be fighting back tears but we all knew this wouldn't be a place to let them flow. Cartel looked real drunk and all he could say was, "Sorry. It's the last time I shot a gun."

———————————

I GREW A mustache to honor Sam Knudsen. He'd had this real bushy mustache, brown and soft and even, just a real enviable mustache. I'd never grown one before and the first few days I had to remind myself that my embarrassment was temporary; Sam Knudsen could never grow one again.

We all grew mustaches; Cartel's was most like Sam Knudsen's. O'Brien's was blond and always looked wet. Greenly's and mine grew in the slowest and we made a contest out of it to see whose would finally come in first. Menser was the only first shifter who refused. We figured he had his reasons. We didn't prod him on why and sometimes when we joked about them and poked fun he'd smile and I could tell he'd wished he grew one, too.

After the services were behind us, Captain Dixon walked into morning muster and told us how much he missed Sam Knudsen. Dixon didn't have any stories to tell about him because the captain hid in his office most days. His idea of mourning was to have a Wiffle ball game in the gym after shift. We'd call it the Knudsen Classic and make it a yearly thing. There was a soft applause that was more sarcastic than appreciative. Because that's what the House did after tragedies. Morale boosters through sport.

We dressed in sweatpants and white T-shirts. All first shifters were there, the librarians and nuns even joined in. Dixon had made the teams himself and we had rules and got real serious about it. O'Brien insisted he pitch; I never would have known he had a wicked knuckler. He sat us down for the first three innings in order and we shagged pop-ups that sometimes got lost in the bright gym lights. Cartel hit a ball so hard it cracked and sputtered in the air, traveled across the large gym, and smacked off the Knudsen Classic banner Dixon had made and strung the length of across the back wall. Cartel ran the bases and everyone yelled. The whole jail seemed to yell.

I lined a ball down to first where Sister Mae was positioned. The ball hit her in the gut and she doubled over like she'd been shot. I dropped the bat but didn't run. Afterward, O'Brien told me it knocked the wind out of her. They were afraid she wouldn't catch her breath. A real heart-stopper, he said. But we'd missed all that; Cartel and Greenly had been tugging at my neck and we used the laughter and commotion to hide the big fat tears in our eyes.

F ield Training Officer O'Brien looked at Officer Candidate Carmichael with acute uneasiness. He wanted to sign him off his leash as soon as possible, get on with his normal work. But he couldn't let this dipshit free to work in his building. He would have to at some point, but not yet. He looked at Carmichael. His fat cheeks bubbled over his collar; the clip-on tie looked crooked and O'Brien couldn't understand how that could be so. Carmichael stood over U3's control panel like it was the controls for nuclear weapons.

O'Brien rubbed his face with both hands and then tried to pull the skin off his forehead. "What's the problem?" he asked.

"When I blink, there's this orb, it's like fluorescent green, and it hovers through my field of vision and currently it is taking more than you can imagine for me not to reach out and swat it away," Carmichael said.

Carmichael's hand danced over the button that opened Inmate Moncrieff's cell. He looked up at the secured unit, then back down at the panel. The kid was on his third FTO and should have been at least break-approved at this point. Carmichael was O'Brien's third too. The House was always running an academy, so O'Brien was assigned an OC every six weeks. He'd only been an FTO for a few months, after he found a shiv on Max. He had been searching the common areas during downtime and noticed, in the shower, an orange knot tied off inside the drain. The drain was loose, and with a bit of urgency he pulled it up and there, hanging by a string of orange fabric, was a blade shoved into a toothbrush. When he brought it to Lt. Hobson, there was no praise. Typical Barker House. Instead, Hobson put O'Brien in for a promotion. It had come too easily, O'Brien had thought. Since FTOs wore brown, same as the officers, same as O'Brien, he always thought of them as honorable representatives of the badge. But having had a few bad candidates, he wondered how any FTO stayed honorable.

"Open the door," O'Brien said. He moved behind the panel next to Carmichael, who smelled like a bag of potato chips.

He turned to O'Brien, his eyes near the side of his face, his pointed ears, his mouth hidden by the cheeks. He looked like a fat-faced rabbit. O'Brien wanted to pick him up by his tail and kick him out of the building.

"For Christ's sake," O'Brien said.

"I hate when that happens. It's like you feel like it's going to rain so you put on a raincoat but then it never rains and the sun's out and you're walking around in a stupid raincoat with this smiling astral ball giving you the look."

O'Brien tried to calm himself. He was genuinely concerned with Carmichael ever working alone in the jail. O'Brien wasn't so much worried he would get himself hurt; he wasn't overly attached to Carmichael personally. O'Brien was actually another what-the-fuck-are-you-talking-about comment away from hurting Carmichael himself. The concern was more about Carmichael fucking up and getting another officer hurt. His body positioning, cowardly demeanor, and who-says-this-shit-anyway type of garbage coming from his mouth. He'd be picked over, laughed at, demeaned, until he surrendered to becoming a contraband mule, or, even worse, their friend.

"Just put your finger on that button right there. It doesn't take much pressure to release it," O'Brien said.

"I find that when I start to feel like this, it's best to formulate an attack strategy. My mother used to tell me, 'Henry, just take a deep breath, count to ten,' but I'd get to ten and ask myself, why ten? Who decided ten was the right number to defeat how *I'm* feeling? Sure, it may work for some people, but there is no way ten works for everyone."

"Hit the button."

"I started trying fifteen and it worked for a while. And then it didn't. So, I switched to twelve, seven, forty-two, and I kept changing up the numbers and the counts to where I couldn't remember which ones worked and which ones didn't."

"I'll just go ahead and do it," O'Brien said.

"I started charting them, the counts. For some odd reason, even numbers worked on a more consistent basis."

O'Brien released the door. He watched the orange-shirted Moncrieff emerge alone into the dayroom. Moncrieff was shorter than Carmichael but just as fat and had long, greasy black hair peppered with thick white dandruff. He stopped in the dayroom, put a hand on his chest, and with his eyes closed let out this high-pitched cry toward the top tier. Moncrieff held the cry for a few seconds before O'Brien walked over and grabbed him by the biceps.

Moncrieff got under the water. O'Brien began a round of the unit. Three cells on the bottom tier were fitted with electrical outlets for respiratory machines, CPAPs, heart monitors. They were the only cells in the building with outlets. Every cell on the bottom tier was a Lexan for close monitoring, and almost every inmate in those cells was wearing a green Velcro dress. A burrito. Officially, a safety smock. He had to walk around three wheelchairs parked outside cells. U3 was a half unit, only twenty-four cells, and because it shared a unit with U2, there was a dividing wall separating the two. It was a normal unit cut in half. O'Brien always thought of it like a two-story warehouse, except with cells, and toilets, and sinks that dripped all night. But now, he imagined it as an old hospital, the way it smelled like bleach and Bengay.

The clear Lexan doors let O'Brien know rather quickly what ailed each inmate. Crutches against the wall, hospital bed, one inmate was perched on his sink, shitting into it. There wouldn't be much sense made of anything down here, O'Brien knew that. It was an infirmary *and* a psych ward, a sub-unit of a sub-unit for the mentally ill inmates. Inmate Sanders barked like a dog in cell 10. Inmate Kilgore stuttered heavily to the point of losing his breath, begged O'Brien to stop and talk to him, asked him if he could buy him a cup of coffee, it was cold out here, he said. Hogan in cell 14 began singing cadence and stomping his feet at his cell door. Hogan was big-chested, his skin white and reflective like waxed linoleum, even whiter and more intense in contrast to the green burrito tied around his waist. His eyes were wild, and when O'Brien stopped at his door to check on him, the eyes widened, and he scowled, raised his hand, and gave O'Brien a salute.

"Did the fat boy tell you he stole my jungle boots?" Hogan asked.

O'Brien shook his head and looked back at Carmichael, who was standing alert but with a blank stare on his face outside the lone shower stall. O'Brien couldn't tell whether he was confident or scared. The guy was senseless.

Hogan's expression seemed almost insincere. He whispered in a raspy voice through the crack in the door and told O'Brien the fat boy stole his boots after he lost his own in a paddy field. Said the fat boy was always crying for his mother, sometimes he even walked off in the night and they'd spend the first few hours of the next day dragging him back. Hogan was animated and, to O'Brien's surprise, spoke well. Hogan continued. He said he liked to sleep with his boots off, made him feel like he was home. Said he didn't care the fat boy stole his boots, they hadn't moved in six days. He pointed over O'Brien's shoulder and said that was him, right there, Carmichael, walking around in his boots. He said he was damn sure they were moving soon and he was hell-bent on getting his boots back.

O'Brien nodded, looked back suspiciously at Carmichael, rubbed his chin, overacted sort of, but Hogan didn't seem aware of O'Brien's sarcasm. O'Brien half wondered if Hogan was pretending himself.

"You ask him about my boots. You'll see." Hogan stroked his long, graying beard. "Carry on, soldier." He turned off away from the glass door, out of the light of the unit, and into the shadows of his cell. His mattress was laid vertically against the back wall, something O'Brien hadn't noticed until then, and he took a boxer's stance in his green skirt and started jabbing the mattress, then sped up his punches until he was in an all-out flurry.

O'Brien was stopped at another cell, this one on the top tier with a regular cell door, red-painted steel with a vertical, rectangular window on the left-hand side covered in a waffled grate. There was a short inmate behind the grate, his face barely visible, barely able to see out of the cell. O'Brien checked his O-report. Iglesias, and he was crying. Iglesias asked O'Brien when he could leave. O'Brien asked him if he meant out-of-cell time.

Iglesias wiped tears from his face. He was very young; O'Brien guessed eighteen. "When can I go home?"

"That's not up to me," O'Brien said.

Iglesias walked away from his door and fell facedown on the bunk. "They told me I could go home." And he began to wail.

Inmates started to yell things at Iglesias. *Pussy. Put him in my cell, I got a shoulder he can cry on.*

O'Brien told Iglesias he'd check on it for him but instead he checked back in on Carmichael, who was still in front of the running shower. He told Carmichael they could do an easy controlled Escape Drill, a 10-13, on U3. They could also do an unclothed search on Hogan after he came out for his shower. Not to overwhelm him, but O'Brien was sure they'd also be able to check off the task of supervising med pass. Carmichael nodded, but didn't show much eagerness or excitement.

"Why do you want to work here? Why Corrections?" O'Brien asked. His tone was frustrated, and O'Brien knew. He was trying to help Carmichael, but there seemed to be no desire in him. The shower kept running with the curtain drawn and Carmichael stared at the curtain with his hands on his hips.

"I always wanted to be a cop," he said.

"This is different. This takes something else," O'Brien said. "I've tried with you. You couldn't be a cop. This is your last chance at being even a CO. You act like someone is forcing you to do this."

"I'm getting married in April. My fiancée found the job posting. I *do* need a job," Carmichael said.

O'Brien pictured Carmichael in a tuxedo, a bow tie wedged under his double chin, standing expressionless as his equally fat fiancée walked toward him in a windowless church, with large women on both sides of the aisle sobbing into tissues. He'd probably found someone who needed him as much as he needed her. Poor girl. Poor Carmichael. Their home would be cluttered, small, dirty dishes covered in pasta sauce, funny pages scattered about the tables. They'd have a bunch of kids, a herd of idiots, tripping over toys, endless laundry, and church on Sundays. He'd coach his sons in football, feel the need to play them even though they sucked. Parents would hate him, urge his removal. His sons would suffer, join the marching band. They'd play the tuba.

"Do the checklist, finish this out. For whoever. I don't give a shit," O'Brien said. He went and sat down at a dayroom table and wrote his round into the pod log.

After Moncrieff finished his tier time, O'Brien gave Carmichael the order to conduct the 10-13. Carmichael immediately went and checked and secured the rec yard, showers, and dayroom and then went cell to cell physically ensuring each cell door was secured. He was doing well, much better than when they tried it on U5, where Carmichael forgot to check the showers and rec yard, and then on his second round he *pretended* to ask inmates to see their wristbands through their grates. O'Brien had snuck up behind Carmichael as he nodded, and seen the two inmates in the cell sleeping in their bunks.

But today's drill went just fine. O'Brien congratulated him on a successful 10-13 and checked off the box on his J-sheet. Carmichael smiled a fat-cheeked smile. He looked around the dayroom at the imaginary accomplishment.

AFTER LUNCH, THE unit enlivened. Hogan did jumping jacks at his door, counting them out in sets of three. Moncrieff sang operatically in gibberish, his arms waving about, his hair standing straight up and swaying like it was in a coordinated dance. Iglesias kept crying, except now he was addressing the inmates who were yelling things at him. "I'm not a baby! They said I could go home!"

O'Brien sent Carmichael around the unit to retrieve the lunch bags from under the cell doors, told him to make sure all the sporks were accounted for. The inmate in cell 1, lying in a hospital bed with a big, loud machine that sounded like a dishwasher, yelled out that there were rats in his bed. Then it was spiders. Carmichael reported there were no rodents and the inmate appeared to fall asleep.

Inmate Sombath lay at his cell door and rapped without taking a breath, a possible attempt at drowning out Moncrieff's stabbing falsetto. O'Brien, and everyone else on the peculiar half unit, knew his name was Sombath, because of a line he kept circling back to, a refrain, but O'Brien didn't think Sombath knew what a refrain was. *And now hear the wrath of Sombath.* He had no teeth and a dark purple bruise on his neck. Every time O'Brien walked by his door, Sombath pretended to reach out, grab at O'Brien's feet.

Sombath sang. *Ever wash out your draws same place you would shit, ever knock push-ups same place you would piss, come feel your girl you're missing her lips, come through for visits she'll sneak you some nips, I know you ain't have a cellmate who went to war with the strip, wake up hear screaming he fighting somebody and shit.* O'Brien didn't hate it.

Carmichael opened cell 14 with less hesitation than he had earlier in the shift. He seemed to be coming around and O'Brien felt that FTO pride, bought into the old idea that anyone could do this job, they just needed guidance. O'Brien went over to the door and told Hogan to put the smock on over his shoulders the right way. Hogan did. His white body was wet with sweat, his black chest hair grouped and fat like fed leeches, and when he walked through the well-lit dayroom he moved like a person of importance, intentionally slow, controlled, with a wide smile spread over his face. An emperor to the bathhouse.

When Carmichael came out of the sally port, Hogan whispered to O'Brien, who was shadowing him, "There's my fat boy."

O'Brien had forgotten about the boots. "Just take your shower, Hogan. I'll talk to him about the boots."

Hogan winked at O'Brien, then nodded at Carmichael like they were old friends. He undressed in the dayroom and folded his smock and laid it outside the shower on the floor. Once the shower was running, O'Brien told Carmichael to stand right outside, make sure he makes no sudden move toward either staircase. Then, O'Brien decided to go try and calm Iglesias.

"Listen," O'Brien said. "This is a pussy unit, but still, if you cry like this in gen pop, they're going to be worse than this. You have to get it together. I have you coming out next. Make a call. Figure your shit out."

Iglesias tried to catch his breath in shuddering gasps but was having trouble. He'd been crying for so long, his body seemed to not want to stop. O'Brien shook his head. He heard the shower curtain rings slide quickly and figured Hogan was finished with his shower. O'Brien told Iglesias to get his shit ready to come out.

O'Brien then turned and looked down off the tier over the railing into the dayroom and saw a naked Hogan standing over Carmichael, who was on his knees and looking up at O'Brien with the shower curtain wrapped around his neck. O'Brien made an Officer Down call over the radio, a 10-44, the first time he'd ever done that, and ran across the top tier. As he started down the stairs he could hear Hogan saying, "Those are my fucking jungle boots, fat boy."

He ordered Hogan to let Carmichael go. Carmichael's glasses had fallen off and his cheeks bunched up in his face, making it look like his eyes were closed, but the pupils were still visible as they tried to move away from the darkness.

"I need them back! We're on the move, soldier!" Hogan yelled and seemed to tighten the curtain around Carmichael's neck. His veiny body was upright, muscles taut; his skin gleamed in mad brilliance.

The sally port door opened via a Central Control override and dozens of officers led by Lt. Hobson filled the dayroom. Hobson came up behind Hogan and put him in a choke hold, then windmilled him to the floor. O'Brien ran to Carmichael and helped him to his feet. Carmichael's uniform was wet from the water droplets on the shower curtain. He tapped at his chest like he was looking for something in his breast pockets but nothing was there. He was breathing heavily.

Hogan was facedown on the ground, two officers were cuffing his legs and hands, and Hobson held his boot on the center of his back. He grunted but wasn't yelling anymore. An officer had slipped and fallen in a puddle of water outside the shower and a few others were helping him to his feet. Hobson looked O'Brien's way but O'Brien ignored the glare.

Carmichael now looked more like he had the wind knocked out of him. O'Brien put his hand on Carmichael's shoulder as he stretched his back and held his face to the ceiling, water pouring out of his eyes. O'Brien knew right there Carmichael was through. He'd be trying another line of work. O'Brien thought about asking Carmichael if he tried finding his happy number while fighting for his life. He didn't ask, though. It hit him that maybe this was his fault. That somehow he had wanted Carmichael to fail. That he should have known better than to leave Hogan with a tubby OC.

And then O'Brien understood. He shouldn't doubt himself; he was unharmed. U3 carried on like none of them saw what happened. Or, they saw very clearly what happened. This is jail. Smiles aren't really smiles but sometimes they are. You just *know*. It takes certain people to understand the world inside these walls. He stopped patting Carmichael's shoulder. Someone on the top tier kicked their door and yelled, "Welcome to Barker House, bitch!" Sombath was rapping loudly over Moncrieff's high pitch; the machine in cell 1 hummed and clanged like a dish was loose, and the wails of a scared kid trickled in as merely a ripple in the noise.

RAY: How hard is it to open a bag of soup?

DON: I was in the shower too long, my fingers are all pruned.

RAY: Oh, man, Don. You woke me up from this magnificent dream. Will you quit it with the goddamn wrapper?

DON: I'm telling you I'm useless. They should take me out back.

RAY: Just bite it.

DON: There. Got it.

RAY: Praise the Lord.

DON: What was it about?

RAY: What was what about?

DON: C'mon, it's the chicken flavor. The chicken one tastes like socks. Your dream.

RAY: Oh, the dream. Yeah. Jesus, some dream. I was in this enormous room. It was really something. All the walls were pastel and there were these Egyptian columns all through the place with lion faces on them. Not structurally necessary but lavish, like freckles on a tit. Way up on the walls near the ceiling were these medieval bookshelves with thousands of books, but all the bindings were the same. This dark red. And there were ladders all over the place crawling up the walls this way and that to the bookshelves. I wanted to climb up there and check out the books.

DON: Ray, you going to want some of this? I promised Paquin I'd bring the noodles and sausage and he's got the crackers. If you throw in some squeeze cheese, you're in.

RAY: You're ruining my damn dream story. Do you even care? Are you listening?

DON: I can do two things at once.

RAY: I'm forgetting most of it anyways. How many times have I told you? Soak the noodles; don't just run piss-warm water on them.

DON: I get grossed out putting food in this sink.

RAY: I just cleaned it. Don, I *just* cleaned it. Those books made me think of my collection. Couple hundred, at least. I scored a first printing of *On the Road* at an estate sale in Vermont. Clean jacket, text was clean, too. Oh, my books. I can only imagine what my illiterate brother is doing with them. I bet that's what this dream was about. All the same bindings. That's it, Don. My subconscious telling me to let my collection go. Never meant anything anyways.

DON: Uh-huh. This brand of sausage makes my fingers pink. Takes days to get this shit off. Looks like I fingered a broad on the rag.

RAY: *Walden, Pugilist at Rest.* Oh, dammit. A signed first edition of *The Stand* made out to "Shirley, the tragic one."

DON: You still telling me about your dream? I'll be honest, I don't care much about books.

RAY: The room didn't just have books in it. Other stuff happened in the dream, it's coming back in pieces. Sure, now I remember this creaking sound like a heavy door opening but I turned all around and couldn't find a door and then I look and then right in the middle of the room there's this great big bed, California king I'm betting, silk sheets; I went straight for it, of course. I ran my fingers over the silk, Don, it was like sunflower petals.

DON: You're dreaming about reading and sleeping, Ray. This place is getting to you.

RAY: Will you let me finish? I'm getting to the good part. On the bed there's this long-black-haired woman spread-eagle. She was young, looked like Linda Ronstadt and her mouth was open like she was about to take a bong hit. But you know that's not what I was thinking.

DON: What *were* you thinking?

RAY: Oh, God, a few things. Her legs were squirming. She really wanted it. It was like she'd been there forever, waiting for me.

DON: You gave it to her, didn't you? You old dog. Now that's a dream.

RAY: Sure.

DON: So, you in on this or what? Paquin's waiting and I saw Ingram drooling over the sausages and I don't want that prick anywhere near this batch.

RAY: Take the cheese from under my bunk. In the box. I'm all worked up now. That dumb fuck probably sold my books on Craigslist. He knows how much they mean to me. It's out of my hands though, right, Don? Give me some consolation here.

DON: It's like me giving away Bernie. He was out of my hands. Now cut it out. At least you remember your dreams. I wish I remembered mine the way you do.

RAY: Don, you should've seen it. The room was enormous.

T he machines beeped and flashed red and green. The man attached to the wires and tubes was still alive, but more than one nurse had used the term "brain-dead." Kelley watched the closed eyelids shudder and imagined the man pleading for a glimpse at the light again. Or maybe only the eyes were pleading, as if they were able to detach themselves from their vessel. Kelley'd been staring at him for too long, attempting to find any signs of life, and every so often the inmate's eyeballs would twitch. The sight before him reminded him of a blind-folded man who had earlier knelt before a firing squad.

The afternoon nurse came in and Kelley tried to look at the ready for critical action, but he and the nurse both knew his presence was not needed. He was merely there for account-ability. Jail policy. She stood over the patient, looked at the monitors, and wrote things down. The man was Inmate Ronald

Henderson. He had hung himself thirty-three days into his stay at Barker House of Corrections. He survived, and they called that lucky. Jail aphorism: *No one dies in our house.* Kelley was reminded of another saying, one that the training coordinator engrained in them as hopeful cadets during the academy: *The inmates leave in the same or better condition than when they arrived.*

"You want a drink?" the nurse asked. "Hungry?"

He told her he was fine, thanks. He smiled. She was overweight, had thick curls in her gray hair. She was nice, smelled like dessert, reminded him of something warm, like apple pie. The comparison made him hungry. He'd last eaten at noon in his apartment, a burnt English muffin that lent itself to being covered in a shitload of grape jelly.

"He could've saved you guys all this trouble," she said, shaking her head while looking down at Henderson. "This overtime for you?"

Kelley didn't know what she meant about trouble. He wondered if she meant it would have been better if Henderson were cold dead when he was found in his cell, or better if he hadn't decided to tie the sheet around his neck at all. He stared at Henderson and wanted to ask the nurse about the eye twitches.

"Was hard to pass up," he told her.

She bent over and fixed Henderson's arms, tucked them closer to his body, as if Henderson had moved them. She looked back up at the machines as if they had changed as well.

"We called his mother. She's up from Florida. This'll be her call," she said. "What's you guys' policy on visits? We've never had one of your boys get a visit before."

Kelley didn't know the policy. This was his first shift ever as a transport officer. He wasn't even formally trained as one. He was sent because the jail could pay him normal overtime, he guessed, not double time like the transport team received. Lt. Hobson gave him strict orders not to talk to any reporters. "Suicides at the House make for good stories. Let's not make this a big thing," Hobson said. "A lowlife went and offed himself and let's not make it a headache." Henderson wasn't going to get up and try to escape. There was no fear of that.

As a rookie, taking on the overtime looked good to a man like Lt. Hobson. It showed Kelley was buying in, ponying up. And it definitely didn't look bad to Rachel. The only reason she minded about tonight was the timing of the shift. Rachel was worried she was pregnant. Worried may have been understating it. When she broke the news to Kelley, she did a rundown of the last dozen times they'd had sex. They both remembered the one time they didn't use a condom. It was after her friend Holly's twenty-fifth birthday, a night of strictly margaritas for the girls to honor Holly's drink of choice, and they were out of condoms. Kelley didn't protest.

"Can I use your phone?" he asked.

The nurse led him to the long counter of computer screens and phones that ran down the entire hallway of the ICU. There were nurses typing, a few talking and eating at the far end, standing around pizza boxes. They looked up at him and he thought about waving but didn't. He was in his brown county uniform, with a badge on his chest, heavy military boots. And it wasn't just his attire, it was what his attire and presence meant to the hospital workers and keen-eyed visitors—there was a criminal among them, possibly a dangerous one. He gave them a nod.

He held the phone and dialed, but each time he hit four digits the other end rang, and he hung up. He didn't know how to dial out and his friendly nurse had hurried off. He did have his cell phone but wasn't supposed to. Calling the House on it would be a dumb move. Instead of looking down the counter to the huddled pizza eaters, he held the phone as if he were successful in calling out. He noticed the hallway smelled sanitized and clean, which had the opposite effect on Kelley, making him feel dirty. The overly clean smell meant a heavy-handed janitor was masking what really lurked about on the surfaces. The jail, on the other hand, stunk badly, a natural stink that made Kelley acutely aware of what lurked about, which he preferred.

A cluster of loud beeps crept out of a room behind him and Kelley turned to watch the crew of nurses parade inside. It was a wild cacophony of bells and alarms signaling a life in the balance. These critical sounds raised Kelley's stress level, reminding him of the brief episode in his life when he spent noteworthy time in a hospital. His grandfather, blind from meningioma, also from the tumor that was killing him, spoke gibberish for three days while fourteen-year-old Kelley wished to be somewhere else other than that bedside: on soft-lipped

Sarah's futon, or playing *Twisted Metal,* or even rolling around the ringworm-infested wrestling room. He could remember his mother's pearl earrings and her breath smelling like ranch dressing when he hugged her. It was in the minute of his grandfather's passing that he felt the weight of the divorce, the absence of his father, in the heavy, flabby arms of his mother.

He decided to try dialing 1 first, which didn't work, then 9, which was how the phones at the House dialed out, and that worked. He was forwarded to Lt. Hobson, who gave clearance for a visit from Gail Henderson. Kelley was instructed to check her ID and her DOB. Kelley was glad he hadn't needed to ask for assistance with using the phone. The nurses appeared to have enough to deal with.

In the single-bed hospital room, there were three large windows on the back wall behind Henderson's head. The shades were pulled to the top. Kelley could see the city outside, the buildings looming in the setting sun, the same buildings that circled the jail that sat in the city's center. The jail did, in fact, look like other city dwellings. Kelley told people he thought it resembled a bank: bricked and inviting. It was as if the architects had that in mind. There was no barbed wire perimeter, no galvanized fences.

Surely a doctor could've relayed the dire condition to Henderson's mother and saved her a rushed trip. She might be the religious type and call in the chaplain and there'd be some prayer or blessing. Even worse, they'd ask him to join hands with them and chant. Kelley couldn't prepare himself to be a part of such a ceremony and he decided once the call was made to turn the machines off, he'd remove the handcuffs and be on his way.

There was also the possibility he'd knocked up Rachel; as unfortunate as she felt that was, he sort of hoped it were true. In one night he could be involved in the end of a life and the beginning of a new one. He checked his phone, half expecting an angry text from Rachel. She could be hotheaded. But there was nothing. She'd said a baby would ruin her body, and at twenty-four she was too young for that. But a weekly box of Chardonnay and late-night lo mein would also ruin a body. Kelley held that quip in. Fatherhood would mean big changes. They'd have to move out of the city, he thought, maybe to Hollis, where they kept their baseball field greens nice and they never made the paper for home invasions. His one-bedroom apartment with the air conditioner fastened in the wall, decent closet space, clean rugs, was enough for him and Rachel. But for a baby, and all the things that a baby needs, the apartment wouldn't do. What was it a baby needed? He thought about this as he pulled down the shades, wanting to give Henderson and whatever visitors some privacy. He knew crib, high chair, maybe a dresser. His mother would be over-the-top excited; even though he and Rachel weren't married, she'd exhaust them with drop-in visits.

He pulled up a visitor chair next to Henderson and sat down. The chair was cushioned and comfortable and he real-ized he'd been standing for over two hours. He stretched his legs and reached for the remote that was on the bed and attached to a cord. His hand brushed Henderson's hairy, cold arm. He expected Henderson to flinch or pull the arm back. When he didn't, Kelley leaned off the chair and inspected Henderson up and down. There was a clear tube coming from his mouth. He was clean, looked nothing more than asleep. Peaceful. His neck was black, almost purple, where the sheet had been tied off. He had a brown mustache and a light beard beginning to sprout around it. His hair was parted to the side, cut short. Kelley thought about how his hair would still grow, still need to be cut. His body would go on: nails needing clipped, bags of urine emptied, the body a siphon, draining feeding bags and filling piss bags, as if unaware of its dire circumstances. The remote was sticky, and Kelley had to press the buttons down hard as he found the five o'clock news.

"News okay, man?" he said to Henderson. "News it is."

The nurse came in on the hour, every hour. She kept the small talk to asking if Kelley was hungry or thirsty. He was, each time he was, but he declined. He didn't quite know why he did that, why he said no to things he wanted. Maybe it was because he didn't want to be an inconvenience. But a drink, a dinner menu, that wouldn't be much. Still, he said no thank you, I'm fine. He kept picturing himself walking through bright grocery aisles at night, looking for the pint of Ben and Jerry's Chunky Monkey that Rachel was craving. He wondered if she would quit her job at Little Minds and stay with the baby, or if the baby would just go to work with her. That'd be convenient.

AT SEVEN THIRTY, he heard the nurse explaining a patient's condition, much like Henderson's, outside the room, and he straightened himself and turned off the TV hastily, tossing the remote onto the bed next to the inmate. He'd been watching a *Chronicle* story about a father who carried his paraplegic son through marathons. He was torn on how to feel about the father. Heroic was his first thought, trudging through those long races carrying his adult son on his back like a limp, giant toddler. But as Kelley focused more on the son during the clips from races, he saw nothing in the son's face, no smile, no determination. His face was as expressionless as Henderson's. Selfish was what it was, not heroic. The father was doing it for himself, possibly began as a self-punishment, but then it became a story, it became about him.

"In four days his condition has not changed," the nurse said.

Kelley stood, feeling he shouldn't be seated. In walked a thin woman with skin so tanned and wrinkled she looked like it were midsummer in Hell and not November in New Hampshire, where there was a chance of snow in the forecast. Her presence brought on a feeling of hopelessness. Of course, he'd supposed the worst for Henderson. But he was accustomed to the comings and goings of inmates: the head count each day dry-erased and changed, additions, subtractions, inmates a part of his life then gone, maybe back again someday, maybe not, maybe crossing paths in public, a nod of recognition in the mall before averting their eyes in embarrassment to whoever accompanied them. But this woman's dreadful hunch made him uneasy about his attempt to be apathetic toward Henderson. The nurse closed the door, closed out the hallway sounds, and then it was only the hum and beeps of machines. Kelley picked at a callus on his palm. Not seeming to notice him, the woman began to wilt, her shoulders slowly depressed until she was almost in a bow, then she seemed to catch herself and she inhaled and inflated and regarded Kelley with a muscled smile.

Kelley introduced himself. He felt apprehensive about asking for her ID but did it anyway. The woman didn't look away from Henderson, reached into her purse, and handed him a Florida license, confirming she was Gail Henderson. She walked forward slowly, her face contorted, as if they had the wrong patient. She finally looked at Kelley as he handed back her ID. She wore a bright-green down jacket, dark-blue jeans. Other than her tan, Kelley wouldn't have been able to tell she was a traveler.

"What did he do this time?"

Her tone was not what Kelley expected. It was not shaken, but cold, like Henderson's arm.

Kelley knew her son was suspected of battery on a woman. Domestic issues. None of his business.

"I think robbery, I'm not sure though," he said. "I try not to know."

"Keep it simple," she said. "The less you know."

She looked at Kelley, her eyes gray like pavement in the desert of her face. She sat down where Kelley had been sitting and turned herself to the bed.

Kelley took a few steps back away from the pitiful reunion of mother and son and stood at the end of the bed. She reached out and held Henderson's hand. He snuck a look at his phone but the home screen was void of messages.

"He was never a good boy," she said, stealing Kelley's attention. "He gave me trouble from the moment he was born. His father wasn't a good man either. There's something to be said about that." She spoke while looking at her son. "You think he can hear me?" she asked.

"Maybe," Kelley said, hoping she hadn't seen him check his phone. He was not sure how involved he should be in the situation. He was not sure really what he was supposed to be doing.

Gail sighed. She sat quietly for a while looking down at Henderson. Kelley felt intrusive. If he could have excused himself, he would have. The mother showing up on his shift was just his dumb luck. He thought about Lt. Hobson's directions. "Sit there and observe. If his condition changes, call."

He watched the woman hold her son's hand and he couldn't tell if she was relieved or desperate. A parent could never know how their child could turn out, he thought. Unless she knew, and this moment had been anticipated, which Kelley concluded maybe it had by Gail's temperament. She was calm, like Kelley's mother had been during the final hours of his grandfather's life. Around noon on the third day, after hours of sobbing, Kelley's mother snapped out of it and began to eat the chocolate pudding cups she'd been saving for when the old man got his appetite back. She had handed one to Kelley and they didn't stop until all the cups were spooned clean.

If he could reply again to the nurse's statement from earlier, he'd say sure, it would've saved everyone the trouble if Henderson was hours old when found. And if Rachel was pregnant, the rest of Kelley's life would be a series of trials he'd always be surprised at. He could never know anything about the future again.

Gail sat in silence for a while. She kept running her hand through her short black hair. Her hair would slick back for a moment, then split down the middle and fall back into its original place.

"How long have you been a jail guard?" she asked over the machines.

He told her a little over six months. He knew her interest was only to relieve the silence of the room. But he wondered what she saw, how she looked at him. He stood watch over her son, clean-cut in his pressed uniform, a living example of what being on the right side of the law looked like. He felt righteous and seemed to stand a bit more upright.

"I was in jail once in Mississippi," she said. "The guards there were pricks, touchy. That was before I had Ronny. My stay wasn't long either and I've never been back to that wretched state."

She looked away from Kelley and he relaxed his posture. She turned her hand over, flipping her son's hand with it—attached to the bed rail by a handcuff—and she looked at it.

"Overkill?"

"It's policy," he told her.

"Institutions are inundated with policy," she said. "In the last twenty-four hours I've had to show my license to four different people in uniforms. Four!" She held up four fingers to Kelley. "Before that I hadn't taken it out of my purse in God knows. Oh, it don't matter."

She looked up at the screens. The machines continued to run and beep and blink like they still had a job to do.

"Who knows what all this is for? You think they even know?"

Kelley shrugged.

"Honey, you got a baby face," she said. "The men in jail must give you damn hell."

Kelley smiled and nodded, mainly to make her feel like she had been right about something. But he thought about it and she was right. Even though most officers got hell, regardless of baby faces, Kelley seemed to get it more than his partners. He rubbed inmates the wrong way. He'd memorized the inmate handbook.

"Do you say words?"

"When I have to, yes."

"I'm sitting here trying to get my mind off what my mind's on," she said. "You could help by entertaining me."

He told her he'd try harder and she turned her attention back to her son. The room was stuffy and Kelley regretted pulling down the shades.

"The things I thought I knew about Ronny, I knew the least," she said. "He had me fooled." She tossed her son's hand onto the bed and turned from him. "Do you do that, Officer Kelley? Do you fool your mother?"

He thought about it. It was a trickier answer than yes or no. Was omission fooling? He wondered about her word choice. If fool meant lie, then yes, he fooled his mother. He remembered a time when he was a teenager and he cursed his mother, called her a bitch—for what, it didn't matter. She slapped him and ordered him into the car. She drove him to the church and sent him inside to confess. He instead sat at a pew and cursed her over and over in the presence of a hanging bronze Jesus, never entering the confessional. He always felt bad about that day.

"I don't," he told her.

Gail looked shaken now and rubbed her face. Kelley imagined her being fooled by Henderson. A phone call asking for money. Cigarettes slipped from her purse. A car wrapped around a tree, Henderson fleeing on foot into the woods. "She hit me *first*," he'd tell her.

"You boys. Bred for lying," she said. She watched Kelley's reaction, which was nothing at all. He suddenly didn't want to play anymore. He wanted his shift to end. He wished Gail would leave. He hoped the nurses wouldn't come in, led by the doctor, with their hands in front of them, solemn but resolved, like heretical blue-scrubbed agents of death.

"Tell me one time you lied to your mother," she said. "And don't lie about lying. I'm not good at seeing a lie."

She wasn't going to give up. As much as he didn't want to be there, he was there. He thought about sharing the confession story with her, but decided on something tamer, something to slow the conversation down. He told her about how, when at college, he asked his mother for money to buy a book for a class but spent the money on beer. He omitted never needing the book to Gail, having stopped going to classes early in his

freshman semester, and failed out the following one, earning
only three credits.

"Please, I wish Ronny did that," she said. "At least he
would've had to have been in college." She sat for a moment
looking at her son, then sighed. "What do I do here?"

"I don't know."

"You're no help," she said and wiped her teary eyes. "Did you
know him? Was he happy or is this really what he wanted?
People do this as a cry for help. That I know. But Jesus, Ronny.
Look at you."

Kelley only worked Henderson's unit for overtime one
night. He remembered Henderson only because of the
mustache and how he walked the tiers with a short Spanish
inmate, hip to hip, talking, like old men exercising in the mall.
In the suicide prevention course in the academy, Kelley learned
most people are at their happiest once they've resolved to going
through with it.

"I met him once," he said. "I couldn't tell either way."

"On the plane I thought this would be easy. But seeing him
laid up, he looks comfortable, almost like he could stay like this
forever."

"I'm sorry, Mrs. Henderson."

"Gail," she corrected with a playful, raised finger. Her eyes
were watering harder now, but she was holding back any real
crying. "Do you think you could give us a moment?"

Gail looked away but Kelley nodded anyway. He left the
room and went out into the hallway. Nurses moved about, and
he welcomed the noise of commotion and quick feet. He called

Rachel. She didn't answer. He hung up and wanted to text her but didn't.

He went back into the hospital room and saw Gail with her arms around Henderson's neck, his head lifted a few inches off the pillow. She didn't see Kelley come in as she rocked her son, cradling his head.

Gail laid Henderson's head back down gently and noticed Kelley standing there.

"Don't ever let your mother think you were something she made up, like she'd mistaken carrying you, mistaken your crying. You make your mother know you're really here," she said, and Kelley couldn't tell if she was talking to him or her son.

"I will," he said. He almost felt like he meant it, like when the lights were off and he drove the county vehicle back to the garage and punched out he'd be sure to reach out to his mother, let her know she'd never been mistaken. He couldn't decide if his mother would tell him that she, in fact, was questioning that very thing. She might say you never call me. I can't smell you in the house anymore. What ever happened to those football trophies you won? I could've sworn I heard you come up the stairs the other night, the way you always skipped a step, but when I came to the door you weren't there.

Gail inspected Henderson as Kelley had. She looked methodical about it, like she was looking for something.

"It's funny. If he didn't do this to himself I might be sitting thinking if he was real or not," she said. "Him dying makes him alive."

Kelley wanted to say again that he wasn't dead yet. But there was no sense in trying to calm her. He knew she wanted him to say something but nothing came.

"I'll stay long enough for the funeral but not a minute more," she said. She laughed clumsily, hid her mouth with her hand, as if the laugh surprised her. "His funeral should be something. Nice and empty. He never let anyone know him. He'd hurt them or run off long before they could. Such a damn waste you were. I could've birthed you straight into a casket and it would've made no difference."

Gail ran her hand down her son's cheek, and then sort of pushed his head side to side. Quickly, she snapped her hand and slapped his stiff face. It startled Kelley, and with another quick fling that seemed to come from her elbow, she slapped him again. Then came an eruption of slaps that made Henderson's body flop on the bed, the green straps coming down his chin, and the machines started to alert disharmony. Kelley ran to Gail and put his arms around her, pulling her away from the bed. She let her body go limp and collapsed to her knees. She felt like merely bones under her jacket, his cheek against her hot cheek like it was still burning from the sun reminded him she was more than just bone. He held his arms around her, and he felt her hand cover his hand and squeeze.

The nurse ran into the room, followed by a stream of nurses directing each other, and they huddled around the bed. Gail was shaking and crying softly in his arms, clutching his hand. He imagined the nurses behind him unplugging the machines, discarding the bags and tubes, changing the sheets, raising the shades, as if Henderson's body were already removed.

Gail rocked in his arms, then swiftly sucked in her breath and stopped her crying, as if she willed it, as if the extent of her mourning were done. She was done with it. He couldn't feel her breathing, couldn't feel her heartbeat through the jacket. Her body swayed as if strung from a pivot. Kelley wondered if Henderson had ever held her like that. If he had ever held her like she were both alive and dead at the same time.

Part III

NUMBERS

Big Mike / Cookie Jar   "*The Mouth*"

C hun-Li was a bipolar Asian girl on Saturday night's JV squad. She stripped where I bounced weekends: the Cookie Jar. Chun-Li was her stage name, a somewhat successful attempt at playing off anime fantasies, coupled with a pubescent sexual attraction to an oriental, large-tittied, thick-legged video game character from my childhood. We'd have drinks after shifts. She'd be done dancing and taking customers by midnight, would sit and drink bottles of beer that looked enormous in her tiny hands. She'd look almost normal in her T-shirt and jeans, normal to most men probably, but tough for me to forget her getup from a few hours before.

I'd join her when I was done clearing the place out, and Tito let us stay until four on most nights, sometimes longer, especially when the college girls were bartending, wanting to collect tips for as late as they could. Chun-Li told me she wasn't even Chinese. Her name was Rosa. Well, not Rosa, but her Cambodian name was too hard to say as a kid so they called her Rosa. She said if her father saw what she did, how she dressed and made money off pretending to be Chinese, he'd kill her. Her father escaped Pol Pot and the Khmer Rouge, carried her sister and sometimes her mother, too, for ten days, from Cambodia to Thailand. That had nothing to do with being Chinese; she'd just disguised a heritage he'd tried so hard to protect.

"My father was a doctor," she told me. "Anyone with an education or glasses was the first to die. He walked almost blind. He falls asleep with his glasses on now—I think, out of spite."

I equated the girls many times to the inmates I watched during daytime hours. They seemed to be somewhere they couldn't find a way out of: drugs, sex, lies. The girls were imprisoned within themselves. I found myself attracted to this self-imprisonment. I had a need to try and save them. I tried it with an inmate once, but it didn't work out. She couldn't keep herself from going upstate, and if they're too far from saving, then what good am I?

I wanted the most for Rosa. I wanted her to tell me what brought her there, what could have been so bad to make her put on that stupid outfit, rub herself on dicks, betray her father's valiant trek. I asked her once one night when we were both a few beers deep—her being able to keep up with me beer for beer should have been a red flag, but I was into it—when was she diagnosed with bipolar disorder. She sat the beer down on the bar. She wore contacts that messed with her eye color, contacts that were chemical-spill blue, blue like porta-potty water. "I was fifteen and out of control. Sleeping around, disappearing. My father pretended like everything was fine," she said. "My mother, she knew. Someone spray-painted *Rosa sucks dick* on the side of a convenience store near my house. My mother had me tested right after."

"How'd she know?" I asked her.

She told me her mother was bipolar. Her father pretended like her mother was fine, too.

We were friendly but not sexually involved. That changed one Saturday night in September. I arrived at the club for my shift. The sea breeze from the Atlantic came ashore in a swirl and wrapped around my freshly shaven head like I'd stuck it in the freezer. I walked through the gravel parking lot sporting the boots that I wore to the jail, the boots also moonlighting at the Cookie Jar. The boots stomped more heads at the club, courtesy of my boss Tito's old-school kick-his-fucking-teeth-in approach to ass grabbers and pussy fingerers.

Outside, I packed a lip, mainly for show. I looked out across from the lot where the demise of the south end beach was apparent: empty batting cages, a darkened go-cart track, a shuttered ice-cream stand, and a carless two-lane highway that seemed to run right into the ocean. The bar next to the batting cages was dark, alternative '90s music coming out the propped-open front door. There were lines of motorcycles parked outside. My lot was full of work trucks, ladders hanging on the racks, toolboxes and wet saws in the beds, dashboards covered in crumpled cigarette packs. The post-summer months brought in the workers, the lower-middle-class laborers and painters, at the beach for summer home repairs and cheap off-season rent.

The beach strip was bare of free pussy, save for some motor-cycle club's tattooed barflies, so the men came to the club hoping for a hard-on to start, and, after a few drinks, a paid-for rub and tug to finish. Some would even beg for an over-the-jeans handy.

I swiped the dip from my mouth and went into the club. It was ill-lighted. I'd actually never seen the place in full light, and I was probably better off for that. The front lounge had a dozen round tables that'd fill up as the evening went on. A long bar was on my right. On the walls were photos of guest dancers, promos framed and signed by porn stars. Jenna Jameson back in '04. Asia Carrera in '05. The place smelled like a wintergreen car-air-freshener tree. Chun-Li was sitting at the bar with her left tit actually *on* the bar. She was drinking a bottled beer, and she sort of tipped it at me when she saw me. I wanted to smile at her. But every time I saw her in the club, I had to remember we were two actors in scene. I nodded at her. There was an Indian man sitting with her. He looked over his shoulder to see where Chun-Li's attention had gone, and he smirked at me. The Indian man was a regular; his name was Arun. He owned a tax preparation business in Salisbury. He always had cash, and he didn't drink, spent most of his time talking to the girls, trying to get them to leave with him. He was rarely successful.

The music was loud. Georgia was bouncing on the stage for a dozen or so patrons seated at the curve of it. She was banging her heavy heels on the black wood, a trick the girls did to make it seem like their pussies made harder contact with the stage than they did. Rosa brushed Arun's arm to excuse herself and made her way over to me behind the DJ booth. DJ Salazar paid no attention to us.

"All I've eaten today is a banana." Rosa rubbed her bare stomach. She had on just the midi skirt from her blue Mandarin costume that Tito ordered online for her act, something he would do if pitched the right idea. Her costume and name were enough for the men who recognized who she was emulating, and her tits were enough for everyone else, which were really something on a petite Asian girl. Rare like an innocent inmate. "Do I look bloated?"

"Not at all."

"I feel pudgy," she said. She didn't have an accent, didn't even try to have one.

"You look great," I told her.

"You must be sweet to everyone," she said.

I knew she was waiting for me to share my coke but she was nice enough to not make me feel rushed. I took the small bag out of my pocket. I sprinkled half my coke on a broken pub table, cut it up and lined it with my county ID. She rolled up a bill and leaned in and did two small lines. Then I cleared the rest. Georgia hung upside down in a full split. Everyone seemed to be behaving themselves.

"I just thought of something, Big Mike," she said, looking like she had just sneezed. "You've never tried to fuck me."

"I respect the workplace relationship too much," I said. We did flirt a lot and she once told me I looked mean, which meant I was a good fuck.

"Try sometime," she said.

Georgia walked between us, hand in hand with a smiling laborer, leading him past the bathrooms to the private stalls. I figured she'd gone behind the stage to get my attention.

"I got to keep an eye on this," I said, pointing to Georgia.

"Find me after." Chun-Li smiled but it was tough to get all cozy and warm inside as she turned away and her bare tits swung with her.

The three private stalls were normally full from ten till two. Men followed the dancers in with hopes of banging them, maybe a blow job, but only the girls who wanted to lose their job did that. The bouncers listened for any signs of funny business. We were pretty strict about it. If guys wanted it that bad, or bachelor parties came with the wrong idea, they could go south a hundred or so miles to Providence and do whatever they wanted to the girls.

Georgia was a redheaded girl who looked like she'd never been in the sun, had tiny tits and bright-pink nipples. She liked her job too much and didn't do the extras. I felt the coke kick in. It heightened the impact of everything. The music, the lights, the dancers—it all seemed to be for me. From underneath the door, I could see Georgia's slinking shadow grinding up the filthy customer, the shadow exiting the stall, covering my feet, coming for me, then being sucked back away. The man grunted a few times and gave a few uh-huhs.

"Mike!" Georgia yelled. "Mike, you out there?"

I pushed the door in and Georgia backed out.

"He tried kissing me," Georgia said.

The guy had on jeans smeared with grease and a sweatshirt that read GARY'S TOWING. He was drunk. I told him to get up.

"It's not like I grabbed her pussy," he said.

"Kissing is worse, asshole," said Georgia.

"Come on," I said and grabbed the guy's shoulder. He told me not to fucking touch him. I had maybe half a foot on him, probably sixty pounds. I head locked his thin neck and pulled him out of the stall. He smelled awful, like marsh sewage. He didn't put up much of a fight. Georgia yelled some more obscenities at him as I walked him out of the club.

I found Rosa in the powder room. She was alone, still in her outfit, texting on her phone. She had another hour of work, maybe two more dances in her. She smiled when she noticed me watching her from the doorway. Some R&B song played on low volume from her phone.

"You caught me," she said.

"Caught you doing what?"

"Being a girl. Come here."

I went to her. I was turned on, highly, and the thought of fucking Rosa in the powder room was unreal. There were mirrors all around, low lighting from the strung-up Christmas lights, and a soft sofa.

"Big Mike, in my arms," she said. We kissed; her breasts were pillowy against my stomach. She took my shirt off. I unbuttoned my pants, and she shimmied them down to my knees, taking my boxers with them. I was afraid I'd get coke dick but didn't.

She went at it for a bit then took her mouth off and stuck my balls in her mouth and rolled them around like they were hard candy. She stopped.

"Is there something wrong with you?" she asked.

"No." I felt myself begin to shrink.

"One of your balls," she said as she retreated back to her chair, "it's hard and way bigger. Like a golf ball."

———————

MY DOCTOR MADE a similar face as Rosa had. She held my balls in her fingertips and scrunched her face, as if she were trying to find out if a peach was ripe. Not concerned, but prudent. There was a problem. She wouldn't need to sell me on it. I spent my entire drive home from the powder room fiasco two nights ago feeling my balls, trying to come up with any reason as to why one was squishy and the other was like my dick had swallowed a rock. I called out of work and avoided touching it again. All I could think of was my dad and what he went through with cancer, much different cancer, throat and stomach. How small he got, exponentially during the span of a single summer, until he was nothing and no longer.

I'd made my own *Law and Order* marathon on Netflix and ordered Chinese food three times. I'd resigned myself to being on a clock I couldn't see, the hands spinning around and around in hyperspeed. I had tried to sleep but couldn't. I kept constructing images of a cosmic hourglass in the sky, just beyond our atmosphere, tilting sideways, something or someone monstrous holding it, laughing at me deeply. I left the dishes dirty, the laundry too. I kept thinking about what the point was. All the shirts I'd ever cleaned, loose bike chains I'd looped back over sprockets, ground balls I'd muffed—what was the point of any of it?

I did shower, though, only because I knew my doctor would be fondling my boys. I couldn't lose all respect.

"Usually, hard is no good," Dr. Smarzda said. Old Russian, no-nonsense. "It's very hard. Like avocado pit."

I sat back on the paper-covered table. She typed with her ungloved hand on the computer. "I'm ordering ultrasound. A urologist will need to examine results."

I studied a poster on the wall: the bones of the inner ear. The illustration looked like a map into the center of the earth.

"Do you hear me, Michael?" She had a face like a nun.

"I do."

"Have you been doing self-exams?"

"I didn't know I had to." I couldn't explain to her how this issue was found. I wondered if the prospect of banging Rosa was all but ruined, if a relationship could begin with me on a death sentence. I hadn't heard from her, but I hadn't reached out either.

"Ages twenty-five to thirty-five what we recommend. Your highest risk years." She typed again. The nasal cavity looked like a moth in a skull with its wings spread.

"Your family have history of cancer?" Her dried old cheeks were wavy like a crimp of wool.

"My grandmother. My father." I didn't want to explain. At this point, I wondered what good it'd do. "When will I have the ultrasound done?"

Dr. Smarzda tore off a piece of paper and handed it to me. "Go to reception desk," she said. "There may be opening today." She removed the glove from her hand and dropped it in the can under the sink. All those wasted gloves.

———————

I SAT IN the ultrasound and radiology waiting area at the Family Health Center in Chelmsford, awaiting my ultrasound with three women who were obviously pregnant, another two who may have been. Only one woman had a man with her. All the pregnant women looked like they needed to be doing something but weren't. One bit her nails while another shook her leg, the nervous anticipation of a new load of worry. Cuddle time. Middle-of-the-night feedings. I didn't really know what they were expecting, but I was trying to kill time. The white-haired receptionist chewed her pen while she held a phone to her ear. There was no fish tank. It wasn't a pediatric waiting room. No one really talked. Everyone just looked down at their phones. The pictures on the walls were faces of famous people on stamps—Elvis and Einstein and Johnny Cash.

I watched a door where I saw a pregnant woman get called in by a nurse. At 1402 hours, a woman came down the hallway behind that door and she called my name: Michael Piccard.

The woman who called me was normal-looking, maybe in her early forties. She wasn't fat or skinny. Just plain and motherly. I put my phone away and followed her down the hall.

She asked me to state my DOB and I did. She led me into a room with a hospital bed, a large computer monitor, and two chairs. It was dark, the only light a metallic green coming off the monitor. The room smelled like plastic.

She had on thick-rimmed glasses and soft-green scrubs, lines on the corners of her mouth—probably a smoker—and her brown hair was up in a loose bun, held in place with a pencil. She spoke intently, directing me to undress from the waist down.

"First time?"

I nodded.

"Cover your genitals with this." She handed me a large paper napkin. "I'll be back shortly." She left and I did as she asked.

I tried to get comfortable but couldn't. I wished I'd taken off my hooded sweatshirt. I looked strange with it on. I flattened the paper on my lap. My father had done something like this alone, too. A tube down the throat, endoscopy. The results given tersely. Stage four. A month too late. What better way to hear it? Like a car crash you survive, only to wake up and be told you're bleeding out, nothing can be done. I couldn't help but wonder if this were the place I'd be given a final notice on *my* tenancy. The screen would turn red, brightly even, and mark the spot where the poison had already been delivered, a faint bite in my sleep, leaving no mark, stealthily taking me down without rush.

When the tech came back in, I propped myself up on my elbows like a bikini-clad teenage girl on the beach. I felt even sillier in this pose but didn't want to readjust so suddenly as to make her aware of my own awareness of my positioning. The tech sat down and didn't seem to notice.

She put gloves on, then took out a tube and squeezed gel onto a tiny probe. "This helps me see inside. I'm going to start with the left testicle first." I braced myself for the probe to be cold but it was warm. As she found my hard testicle, I was surprised my penis sat limp on my thigh.

"Yep, you're the one giving him trouble," she said to my testicle.

She rolled the probe around and snapped photos on the monitor by tapping a key. She kept her focus on the screen, taking dozens of photos, and I leaned forward to see if I could spot anything strange in them. They just looked like white walnuts floating in space.

"It feels almost like the size of a kumquat." She typed a few words, and I believe she typed exactly what she had just said, proud of the comparison.

"Is it cancerous?"

She took a few more photos. "I'm not supposed to say. Moms ask, 'Is it a girl?' Fathers ask, 'Is it a boy?' I'm not supposed to tell."

"But you know?"

"Fifteen years of doing something makes you an expert in my book. But I'm just a technician. The final say comes from the white coats."

"Okay. So will I live?" I smiled as if the question were more like "Fries or mashed?"

" 'Is that a penis?' The fathers always see a penis." She clicked some more.

"This is a bit more concerning than a gender reveal." I didn't mean to come off as rude.

She lifted the probe and wiped it on the paper on my lap. The probe nudged my penis.

"The results go directly to the urologist."

"How about a thumbs-up or down?"

She stared at the pictures on the screen, and then released an aggravated sigh. "I had a father once, a husband, I believe, I actually can't remember. Whatever, that's not the point. He begged me to tell him the sex. Like I said, no expert here. His wife kept saying, 'Cut it out. It's too early to tell. Leave the poor woman alone.' I was really holding it in. And she was sort of right; it was a bit early. He was leaning over me, pointing at the screen. His wife was mortified. Tiny little thing. Her belly looked like she wasn't even pregnant." She dabbed the probe in the gel again. "They started arguing. He told her it better be a boy. He did everything, cut out soy, tap water, he worked out. She kept telling him it was up to God. You know what he tells her?"

When I realized she was waiting for me to answer, I asked, "What?"

"If it's not a boy, he doesn't want it." She stared at me in disbelief, her thin eyebrows raised, and in that moment she looked like my mother watching the evening news, commenting on the constant evil in the world. "We live on a volcano," my mother would say. "It's raining knives. They use crockpots as bombs."

"What a dick," I said. My penis remained slinked on my thigh. "Was it a boy?"

"If there was a penis there, I didn't see it," she said and began probing again. "Sometimes it's too early, I get a bad angle, whatever. I'd rather not be the one to change someone's life because I don't have the answers that would come next."

As she kept taking pictures and finding new angles, I thought about how my entire life would change. They'd remove the testicle, maybe I'd have them put it in a jar, stick it on my mantel. I'd get a fresh start on life, just a bit lighter on my left side. A positive result might just be what I needed, a funny story Rosa and I would tell people when asked how we met. "Oh, wait until you hear this one. I saved his life," she might say.

"You hear that?" she asked, giving me a quick jolt with the probe.

There was a *therrrump, therrrump* coming over the monitor. "What is that?"

She stopped probing. "Your heartbeat."

———————————

THEY SAID THE urologist rotated between Boston and Chelmsford, so it could be three days before I heard anything. I didn't tell my mother and I didn't tell anyone at the jail. I worked my shifts like nothing was wrong, like I wasn't daydreaming on the tier, mentally compiling a bucket list: Camden Yards, Ireland, anal.

I went to the club on Friday, still without a result. Rosa came up to me right when I walked through the door. I was afraid she'd ask me about my golf ball.

"Have you seen Tito?" she asked me. She looked concerned and rubbed her arms like she was cold. She had on her Mandarin skirt with no top again.

"I just got here," I said.

"What about Georgia? I've done three straight songs," she said. She looked around the club. Arun was at the bar and a few guys were drinking but no one was sitting around the stage. It'd fill up soon, though.

"Like I said. Just got here. I'll find them."

I did a lap of the lounge, asked the bartender if she'd seen Tito—she hadn't—and decided to go check in his office. My partner Paul would be in at ten and would be asking about Tito too. Tito's office was behind the stage to the right, on the opposite end of the hall where the powder room was.

After I knocked, I heard something slide across the floor, or a drawer slam, behind the door, even over the bumping house music. Tito didn't answer. I knocked again. The door swung open. Tito stood there, his face sweaty, his suit jacket off, and his shirt unbuttoned, revealing blacker chest hair than I would have imagined.

"Get in," he said. He closed the door behind me. On the floor, in front of his desk, lay Georgia. She was on her side, her legs gently moving across the carpet. She was dressed in green lingerie, top and bottom. On the black rug, she looked even whiter, sickly.

I knelt beside Georgia and brushed her hair from her face. I asked Tito what happened.

"She's overdosing, Mike. What the fuck does it look like?" Tito raked back his hair with his fingers and looked at me with surprise, like he'd been the one who just walked in. His hands and nails were manicured, his face smooth and gray, the skin of a man who used lotion and cleansed. He tried to quell his own anxiety by attempting his affable laugh. He was too intentional.

"Heroin?" I asked.

Tito nodded.

"You too?"

He shook his head. He told me he was going to but Georgia wigged out after she shot and wouldn't talk or nothing.

"She been using for long?" I asked.

"Sure," he said.

I looked around the office. His desk was clear, the yellow leather couch looked clean. The sound I heard must have been Tito hiding the evidence. Strip club owner, heroin user. What was the desire to own a strip club? At what point does a man make such a business decision? And yet I also chose to work at one, and for not much money. I enjoyed the role I was able to assume. I liked seeing Rosa and throwing my weight around. It was good for stress. Maybe Tito liked having the girls whenever he liked.

I studied Georgia. She looked peaceful, her mouth almost in a smile. I thought about how easy it'd be for her to leave, to go away, to just drift off without a fight. I was sweating and thinking. Overdoses happened often on U2, the Classification Unit, the first stop for inmates on their way in. If they had a stash, even remnants of a nest egg tucked in a cavity, it was drained within hours of incarceration. Overdoing it was commonplace, so, as we did with fire extinguishers, we did with

Narcan. If she'd been using for long, she might have some skag serum.

"I'll be right back," I told Tito.

"Do something, Mike!" Tito yelled.

"I am."

I ran out of the office. Rosa was onstage. I went to the side of the stage and called her. She stopped dancing immediately and jumped down.

"You find them?" she asked. Her neck had drops of sweat on it. Her eyes looked like she knew what I was about to tell her.

"Does Georgia carry Narcan or something like it?"

Rosa looked down at the ground. "We all have a kit."

"Get me it," I said. "Anyone's."

Rosa went behind the stage to the powder room. *We?* Rosa was using too, and not to be judgmental or anything, I had my own issues, but the needle was a bit beyond my acceptable drug usage. A song still played but no one was onstage to dance to it. The half dozen patrons didn't seem to care. They drank at the bar.

Rosa came back holding a gold handbag down near her crotch. She gave it to me and I opened the bag and looked through. Inside were a few tampons, a condom, bobby pins, and underneath all that, a yellow-capped plastic syringe. I wasn't angry with Rosa for being a user, instead it added to my affinity for her. She was in a bad place.

We hurried back to Tito's office. He was sitting on the couch with his face in his hands. Rosa said something about God.

I got on the rug and rolled Georgia on her back, uncapped the syringe, stuck the white cone in her nose, and released the Narcan into her nasal cavity.

"Give her five minutes or so." I looked up at Tito. "Call 911."

He shook his head. "I can't. I'll have to shut down for the night. I can't afford that. No."

"Are you for real?" Rosa asked.

"Don't fucking talk to me like that. Get the fuck out," Tito said and waved a dismissive hand at her.

Georgia's breathing ramped up, and she picked at the carpet with her index finger. Rosa didn't leave.

"Both of you, out!" Tito said.

"What were you going to do," I asked, "if I didn't come in? Just let her die?"

"I say she's fine," Tito said, his accent pouring on thick in the heated moment, with an added emphasis on *say* and *fine*.

I put my hand on Rosa's back as we left the office. Tito slammed the door shut behind us. There was a part of me that wanted to go back into the office and demand he call, another part of me that said maybe I should just call. I didn't feel compelled to do either. I wished I wasn't so comfortable with people in distress: suicide attempts, beatings, drug overdoses. I wished I wasn't numb to that. I wondered if I'd feel more empathy, feel more badly, for a socialite on her yacht, soaked and cooked in sun, her skin red and bubbling. If I'd feel more for *her* plight. Or a paperboy shortchanged by a customer— would that be worse to me than where Georgia was? What about mine? Had I a plight? Not yet. I had a meddlesome problem that hadn't quite elevated to desperate news but the uncertainty was overwhelming my future forecasts.

I went with Rosa to the powder room. She washed the makeup off her face all the while bitching about Tito. *He's a cunt. A cocksucker.* She looked prettier without makeup. She changed into her casual clothes of a pink zip-up hoodie and tight jeans, a butterfly stitched into the back pocket. She put her hair up.

"I can't do this anymore," Rosa said. "Tonight's been exactly what I needed."

"I hear you."

"Let's go on the beach. Let's get a bottle of something, just me and you."

I nodded and her mouth went wide.

The club was starting to fill up, the girls were being circled, smiling as if willingly ready to be devoured, but their side-glances at me as I walked by them was a reminder that this was all a game where men were pulled to the gates of Heaven but not allowed in.

I saw Paul with his elbow on the bar, keeping a close eye on Arun, who was stroking a girl's black hair. DJ Salazar told everyone to give it up for the Mouth from the South, the freckled firestarter, Miss Georgia. They did. He didn't know Georgia wouldn't be joining. Tito came out of his office and walked over to the DJ booth.

We made our way through the men who laughed and stuck money in their mouths. White lights crisscrossed the stage, then ran through the lounge and back behind the stage. Another dancer climbed up the pole with no introduction.

The bar had three shelves of liquor bottles. A red fluorescent light poured brightly over the top shelf of bottles before it diluted and failed and left the bottom shelf dark. The bartender sprayed soda and tilted a bottle of rum into a glass. She chewed gum and had pigtails. Her stomach was exposed, compact and lined with soft muscle. A man leaned over the bar. She leaned in, and he whispered into her ear. Paul was distracted simultaneously by a group of rowdy college kids and Arun's stroking hands. Rosa walked over to Arun.

"He's got a tiny dick," she told the girl with him. "Real tiny."

I grabbed a bottle of liquor from the bottom shelf and grabbed Rosa. We went out into the night, where a motorcycle dragged by us with a gurgle as we hurried across the highway, past the batting cages and motorcycle line toward the beach.

THE MOON WAS bright and had turned the beach gray. Our feet sank in the sand like it was freshly poured concrete. The air near the ocean was much colder than at the club, almost like they were two different geographical regions. The beach was empty. I gripped the bottle and held it up to the moonlight.

"Banana schnapps?" Rosa asked as she rose onto her toes to read the label. In her closeness I could smell her. She smelled like the shampoo section at Target, the aisles I never had to go down. She bumped me with her hip playfully, hitting me on my thigh.

"It's a bottle of liquor, and we just quit our jobs. Do you really care what it is?" I was disappointed too.

"No. And we quit our *night* jobs. We still have day jobs."

"Lucky us for that," I said and unscrewed the cap and took a whiff. "Holy shit. You first." I handed Rosa the bottle, and she grabbed it with both hands. Her weight shifted forward like I'd handed her a sandbag.

"Pussy," she said. She drew it to her mouth and took a long sip, coughed, then handed the bottle back to me. She shook her head and her small hands retreated into the sleeves of her hooded sweatshirt like a hermit crab.

"I didn't really like the job anyways," I said. "I was always distracted from getting real productive work done."

She laughed. "It's funny where we end up, isn't it?" she said while looking out into the black ocean. With the moon high above us, the water mixed with the sky smoothly like they were one. If it weren't for the sound of waves, we wouldn't know the water was there. "When I was a girl I wanted to be a doctor, like my father."

I'd never heard her sound regretful before. She was always sure of her decisions, however bad they were. I swallowed my swig, the liquor tasting like soured banana bread. Rosa's hands slithered out of the sleeves and welcomed the bottle again. She took another sip.

"What stopped you?"

"Tito got me hooked on H. I bet you didn't know that," she said and didn't pass the bottle back to me. "He gets all the girls hooked on shit."

I got quiet. I thought about my father, all the things I never asked him. What I wondered most about him was how he was with women. I knew the story of him landing my mother but I also knew the ending to that story. What I wanted to know most was his failings, the ones who got away, the ones he mistreated. I wanted to know my father outside of what was traditionally passed down from father to son. It was tough to learn about love from a success story.

"What happened with your thing?" she asked. She looked down to my crotch with a nod.

"It's under review," I said.

"I hope you're okay," Rosa said and single-arm hugged me around my waist.

Sure, I was okay, but my being okay was illusory, a misguided affirmation my world wasn't plunging toward abyss. I didn't say that to Rosa. I didn't want to ruin our noble escape.

"I'll be fine," I said. "It's Georgia I'm worried about. And you." I took out my phone and while Rosa watched me, perplexed, I called 911. I reported the overdose, where it happened, in plain, concise English, like I was writing a report at the jail. Just the facts.

Rosa looked up at me and I wanted to kiss her but didn't. We kept passing the bottle, trading sips, and we talked. I let her talk mostly. If she weren't a stripper, she'd be a normal twenty-two-year-old woman who enjoyed cocaine and sex and not sleeping. She worked days at Merrimack College for the food service company Sodexo. She made breakfast sandwiches for hungover undergrads. She didn't call them undergrads, she called them rich dickbags. She was allergic to fish. She was in love once, but he didn't know it.

"I wanted to be a cop. Statey, maybe. I settled for a dirty jail guard," I said. "How long does it take for an ambulance out here?" I could stay on that beach forever.

"You're my hero," Rosa said with a hint of mockery. She passed the bottle and sat on the sand. She took her ponytail out and the wind blew her hair in wild swirls. I sat down next to her. My stomach wasn't enjoying the banana schnapps, and I couldn't imagine Rosa was enjoying it either. We were exercising some ritual as old as the beach sand. We wanted to comfort each other, share a taste of some familiar indulgence, find something of value like a beachcomber, something worth keeping, even if only for a short while.

"The H didn't stop me from doing anything but being a good dancer," she said. She drew something in the sand with her finger and looked at me, her fake eyes like blue half shells washed ashore. "I saw my father's struggles here. For a long time I didn't believe his stories about his old life."

I didn't know what to say. I should have told her what I'd been thinking about, my own problems and follies, but I enjoyed the sound of Rosa's voice in between the crashing waves. We sat quiet for a few minutes and drank from the bottle. It was almost empty and I was waiting for the buzz to hit me. Rosa didn't look at me. She just stared out toward the water. I was cold.

"He mixes paint cans at Walmart," she said. "Maybe settling is worse than failing."

I thought she might cry so I set the bottle down in the sand and kissed her. Her mouth was tiny and wet, her tongue dabbing like a minnow on your toes. We lay back together in the cool sand and I wouldn't have minded if the water came to us in a freak wave and pulled us in.

Kelley / Booking Department   *"Assigning Numbers"*

T he current Booking officer, Lopez, was retiring. Twenty-
two years was enough, he'd told Kelley, plus the five years
of military time he bought out. *Smart fucking kid I was*, he'd
said. His son was breaking all the rushing records at a prep
school up north. He spoke about his son often, some of the only
times Kelley saw him smile. Kelley was going to be Lopez's
replacement. He studied Lopez's movements, the way he talked,
the new jargon, how he dealt with outside agencies. There was
more consequence in Booking, like control of a door leading to
the sidewalk, for one. Sitting high behind that counter gave him
new perspective. He could see the inmates' alleged crimes, the
disgusted faces on the transporting officers who charged them,
their grungy street clothes. Lopez owned that perspective.

When Rachel ghosted him, Kelley took over the lease and
removed everything from the walls—pictures of the two of

them in friends' wedding photo booths, Dr. Seuss hats and all; a metal crescent moon hung by a screw from the hallway's popcorn ceiling; a chalkboard Rachel used as a dinner menu; a sunflower painting from her girlfriends' wine-and-paint night—and put it all in a box in the bedroom closet. The pregnancy was unfortunate. Losing the baby wasn't.

Lopez was down to his last few days. Kelley felt confident he could slide right into Lopez's chair and snobby demeanor. In Booking, they had a duty to set the tone for a newcomer, or bestow a lasting reminder on one leaving. *You don't want to see this mug again.*

At three P.M., right before the senior citizen sheriffs pulled the court vans in, they got a call that a teenage murderer was en route. They'd figured. He had already allegedly confessed when in custody, was getting heavy airtime as all the networks and radio stations broke into programming to detail the brutality of the murder, the upscale town of Milford where it occurred, and the profile of the victim, a six-year-old blonde girl named Holly, entrusted to the murderer's care. Hobson gave a stay-in-place order over the radio. Kelley corralled inmates into the large holding tank, their faces pressed against the glass. The inmates were curious, asking what was up and "Yo, am I still gonna get out today? My girl's coming." Lopez was amped up, cracked his knuckles. One last go. Tully slid on his leather gloves, the ones he wore to avoid needle pricks during intake pat-downs. They swept the floor, making sure no one was left unsecured.

"I'm going to miss shit like this," Lopez said.

Two young Milford cops handed the new arrival off at the carport door to Tully and Lopez. Though it was December and icy out, the kid wore a hospital johnny, his clothes likely made into evidence. Kelley watched the cops slide their guns into the weapon lockers in the carport. After a pat search, Lopez and Tully dragged the kid across the floor to the safety cell, the one with the Lexan door, and left the kid in there on the floor. The inmates in the large holding cell watched and banged on the glass. Lopez banged back and told them to fuck off.

Then it was quiet.

"Go stand there and watch him," Lopez said. Kelley stood outside the glass. The kid squirmed on the floor, the weak light hid his face. He'd been beaten, definitely.

"Notify Medical," Lopez told Tully as he typed on a computer behind the counter. Lopez exchanged paperwork with the cops. The procedure seemed routine, but the cops were hyped up, as was Lopez, running on autopilot as he rolled the chair along the counter, stapled paperwork, and then hurried back to typing. A one-man assembly line.

"Nurse Jen says to flag him," Tully said. "She saw the news."

"It was a fucking massacre," one cop said. He looked back at the door and leaned down to see inside. "He cut off all of her toes and fingers. Jesus—"

"Joe," the other cop said.

Lopez didn't stop typing. Tully shook his head. The kid's eye was busted and purple. There was a laceration that began at his eyebrow—dark and wet with blood—and curved around his eye. Kelley figured the cops used their cuffs as brass knuckles. Not advised. Kelley had seen his co-workers stick to places hidden by clothing. A karate chop to the nutsack during a pat search could drop just about anyone and make a solid point. Underneath that johnny, Kelley bet, were the beginnings of bruises. If asked, the boy would say he was having trouble breathing. His stomach hurt worse than his face, he'd say. His mother would hate to look at him.

This made Kelley think of the only time he'd abused an inmate. A kid on U3 flooded his cell and they made him choke down a good amount of it. Kelley had driven home in silence that night, thought about working in the new Amazon warehouse.

"He resisted arrest?" Kelley asked the cops.

"He did," they said together.

"We found him walking down the street all bloody," one cop said. "Cool as shit."

"When he saw the lights he ran," the one named Joe said. "Luckily we got him in the woods behind a house. Squirmy fucker."

Kelley wanted to call bullshit but didn't. It wouldn't have accomplished anything. The COs and cops had a tense relationship and it wasn't the typical stepping-on-each-other's-toes type of thing. Mainly, it came from jealousy on the COs' end. Kelley had tested at a few PDs. But without a connected father or uncle or military time, one's law enforcement career was whittled down to a few choices, mall cop and CO being the top options. COs were envious of the good pay, the work details, carrying a gun. As glamorous as it was walking the shit-stunk tiers, serving hard-boiled eggs to skinners, searching come-covered shower stalls, it'd been a dream for many screws to be a cop, Kelley included.

The new admit groaned and tried to stand, but just crawled across the closet of a cell, then lay on the metal bench. The two cops took the papers they needed. Joe gave the small holding cell the finger on his way out.

Kelley stood watch while Lopez cleared the large tank. None of the inmates inside were dressed for the cold outside. The ones coming in might welcome the stuffiness, for a time. "Copley!" Lopez called, and a small cheer for inmate Copley came from the tank.

Lopez came out from behind the counter and stood next to Kelley, smelling like bad vodka. He'd been noticeably hungover all shift, but what was new. "Shit turd. Scum. He needs to be fingerprinted."

"I know."

Lopez coughed into his hand, a wet cough, checked his hand to see if he'd left anything, and then re-tucked his brown shirt into his pants in the front. "I know you know."

Kelley and Tully handcuffed the kid without a struggle. His face was puffy. Kelley couldn't make out the color of his eyes. They carried him by his biceps just off the ground, down the hallway, past the bondsmen's window and the Property Room and then into the Fingerprint Room. There was a camera mounted on the wall, one of six in the Booking department alone. Eyes all around and they knew it.

Kelley un-cuffed the right hand while Tully kept control of the other. The kid had long, thin fingers. His skin was smooth and untarnished. Lopez stood close to him, observing Kelley, and they could all smell Lopez's breath. Kelley rolled the thumb on the fingerprint pad, and then pressed the thumb to the print sheet. Thaddeus Hundley. Eighteen years old. Five ten. Hundred and twenty pounds. Caucasian. Thirty-One Davis Road, Milford, NH. No prior record.

They sat him in the plastic chair bolted to the wall. Lopez asked Thaddeus some intake questions and filled in the answers on the form. Gang affiliation—none. Suicidal—no. Afraid for your safety—no, sir. Hurting a child put him in protective custody no matter what the answers were.

Lopez held up a small digital camera. *Smile*, he told Thaddeus. Once the nightly news got ahold of that mug shot, Kelley thought, Milford PD would have some explaining to do.

THE PROPERTY ROOM was camera-dark. Other than the Bubble, it was the only place in the jail that wasn't recorded. The inmates needed privacy during strip-outs, but that left the room a good place to lay a beating. Lopez and Tully stood in front of the naked Thaddeus. He looked like a Thaddeus, Kelley thought. He had swollen, young eyes, wet with tears. He was a skeleton rolled in cheap cigarette paper. His hair was curly and bright red and glowed like blood on a tissue. He had a tattoo on his left forearm: *Unfollow me*.

"You tough because you can cut up a little girl?" Lopez asked, his nose against Thaddeus's cheek.

"I want to see how tough he is," said Tully, still wearing the leather gloves. He scratched his upper lip.

Thaddeus's hands cupped his penis and he shivered. They'd just seen inside all of his holes. He'd rinsed in the shower beside them. He was now suitable for his stay at Barker House.

Kelley hurried into the uniform closet in the back of the Property Room, behind the racks of black bags filled with inmates' belongings: shoes, court clothes, and intake clothes. Kelley couldn't find a small uniform. The tops and bottoms were thrown all over the floor; he picked out a faded orange top and a newer-looking pair of pants. He guessed a size nine for shoes. Kelley decided that when Lopez was gone and he took over Booking, he'd find time to match all the shirts and pants together, neaten the place up. He rushed back to the front of the Property Room but he was too late. Thaddeus was on the floor.

"If you were a pigeon," Lopez asked, "and I stepped on you, would you know how you sounded?"

The term "fetal position" was loosely used in incident reports when inmates were found overdosed or beaten, but Thaddeus was in the actual fetal position, like he'd crawled back up into the womb. He was chewing his knees.

Lopez lifted his black boot and stomped Thaddeus's face, right on his cheek, just below his already destroyed eye. Kelley doubted Thaddeus had taken Lopez's question seriously.

Even if he had, he probably wouldn't have known how it sounded.

Lopez knelt on his neck. Tully put his bootheel to Thaddeus's face and dug in.

"Enough," Kelley said. His chest tightened and he felt like he'd just been in a fight.

The room was quiet and they all looked at him, even the kid on the floor. Thaddeus wasn't making a sound.

IN THE VACANT sergeant's office, the Booking officers filled out informational reports, corroborating each other's report by reading and writing them together at Lopez's lead.

"Injuries observed upon arrival," Lopez dictated, "left eye contusion, two-inch cut on chin, swollen cheeks, cut on right eyebrow . . . what else?"

"A boot mark on the right side of his face," said Kelley. He waited for Lopez to look up at him, but he didn't.

"We can't write that," Tully said.

"No shit," said Lopez. He was sitting on the sergeant's padded desk chair, hunched over his report. Tully and Kelley sat across the desk on flimsy chairs and wrote on clipboards. The blinds in the windows were open. The Booking department, at 2015 hours, was empty, the lights dimmed. The Bruins were losing 2–1 to the Islanders on the sergeant's clock radio. Yesterday's vodka permeated from Lopez.

"You know you can't write stuff like that in these reports, right?" Tully asked Kelley.

Without looking up again, Lopez said, "He knows that."

"That little prick cut off her toes," Tully said, focusing back on his report. "Imagine being her father."

Kelley could try. Just the night before, Kelley had laid on the soft carpet of the nursery in his apartment, staring up at the wobbly big-box-store crib and dresser. He'd hung up a stitch-by-number his mother had made when she was pregnant with Kelley, a goofy cartoon depiction of Noah's Ark, with big-headed lions and short-legged giraffes. The nursery was a good place to make him feel empty. He'd watched the night-light project fluffy sheep on the ceiling to the tune of "Row, Row, Row Your Boat." It would've been nice, he thought, as he did most nights while alone, to be a father. But he couldn't imagine being the dead girl's father.

"I'd call him a pigeon and stomp his face," Kelley said. Lopez's five o'clock shadow was thick. His cheeks had a rosy tint.

"Kelley seems to take issue with how shithead was handled."

"We barely did anything," said Tully. "Milford did all the work."

"You're right. He looked fine on his way upstairs," said Kelley.

The Bruins tied it up on a power play goal and Lopez put his ear to the small radio. "Booking—in all its glory—is a machine, a mini jail. You can start off a saint. But you won't stay one," he said.

"I can't hit someone who can't hit back."

"You're being funny, right?" Tully asked.

"No, he has a right to feel this way. I did—for a time."

"And now you're okay?" Kelley asked.

"I pretend they are all the same," Lopez said. "That every inmate is the same inmate. I don't want to keep doing the animal comparisons, but hell, it's the easiest way to explain it. It's like every squirrel you've ever met or seen or run over is like every other squirrel. There's nothing that makes them different from the last one you came across."

"It's that easy," Kelley said.

"I can't fucking believe this guy."

"I totally get it," said Lopez. "This place will change you. If it doesn't, you won't be a part of it."

Kelley took that more as challenge than threat. "You know policies, procedures, what we were trained to do, I'll stick to that."

"Oh, grow up," Tully said.

Lopez shook his head. "This is the system."

THERE WERE THINGS that bothered him about Rachel when they lived together. She used to wait until they went to bed to run the dishwasher. The rattle of plates, water spraying from a hose, the old dishwasher banging and humming. He hated that she did that but now he missed it, the quiet while he tried to sleep was worse than the dishwasher. Sometimes he wished he lived next to a skate park, or the commuter rail. But he realized he was capable of running the dishwasher unsuitably at night.

Bachelorism slowly regained the apartment. The coffee table was covered in Powerade bottles, some a quarter filled with brown dip spit. The apartment smelled minty, but disagreeably so. Dunkin' Donuts straw wrappers were balled up and tossed on the rug. Kelley had used a pizza box as a trap to catch a mouse. He wasn't sure if he'd caught it or not. He was afraid to open the box. But he hadn't seen the mouse around. If he took a shit that left skid marks on the toilet bowl, he didn't scrub them off. Not immediately, especially if they were faint and he could just pee them away later. He was happy to watch college football all day and eat entire bags of pistachios and stack the shells into a mound.

While on his day off, he ordered chicken wings online because he couldn't be bothered with having to call. After he placed the order, his phone rang. It was the wing place confirming his order. Angry at their process, defeating the purpose, he told the young girl, no, he didn't order. As if Rachel could sense the squandering of his days off, he received a text from her. *Call?* Please.

"Is he on your unit?" she asked. "Laura had Holly in preschool. Holly's mom won't talk. Like, went mute."

"I'm off the units," he said. He didn't expect it, but he couldn't stand the sound of her voice.

"So you haven't met him?"

"Sort of," he said.

"Did it bother you to have to look at him?"

"I didn't think about it," he said. "He's just another inmate."

"That can't be true. Not with what they're saying on the news."

Rachel hadn't reached out to find out how he was doing. She had a point of contact for what anyone wanted to talk about.

People asked about Hundley. Kelley's mother had called shortly after the murder. "There's a special spot in Hell for that piece of, well, crap," she said. "They should castrate him." Her voice was as angry as she'd allow it, like when he was benched in Little League for the less talented coach's son. "That man's a know-nothing. And with that big belly. He's quite frankly embarrassing," she had said of the coach.

A week ago, his cousin Joey texted from Fort Carson. "Made the news out here. Take care of that."

How was he supposed to explain Hundley to Rachel? What was it he could say for her to reply: *I'm coming to see you.* He understood the outcry. Even the old Greek lady cashier at Market Basket was telling the woman in line in front of Kelley Hundley should be shot. "Something wrong with that boy. Like a rabid dog." She put her wrinkled finger to her head and made a gunshot noise.

"You missing me?" he asked.

"I can't stop thinking about the little girl. She must've been so scared."

"I know. Not how anyone should die. Especially a child."

"Someone should've been there to protect her."

"Too late now." An apartment door slammed in the hallway. "Can't protect everyone."

"I'm sorry things got weird," Rachel said. "I don't eat much anymore, if that makes you feel better. I started smoking again. My mother and I are at each other's throats. She doesn't shut up. Ever."

"We beat him," he said. "The murderer. We beat him so bad his eye almost fell out."

"Liar. You wouldn't do that."

"I could do it."

"You're sensitive."

Six weeks into the pregnancy, three days after the nursery setup, Rachel told Kelley she had a procedure. She wouldn't call it anything else. She wouldn't put up with his yelling, or how he called it an abortion. She hated that word.

A few nights later, Rachel filled a wine glass to the brim and sat cross-legged on the couch. She'd tied up her brown hair and wore a V-neck with no bra, showing off her tanned neck and chest, and put on a house hunting show. She took a big sip and looked relieved. She even sighed. He couldn't believe it was nothing to her, how she could not mourn. He'd never seen her cry. She never apologized.

"She would've had a birthmark on her lower back," he said. "She would've liked softball. She would have been ticklish on her feet but not in her armpits."

"Who?"

"The baby you took."

"It wasn't anything yet," Rachel said. "I can't have a normal conversation with you? You need to move on. It's weird that you can't move on."

Kelley was quiet now. He wanted to make her suffer but realized there was no way he could.

"You still there?" she asked.

He waited for Rachel to hang up, but she didn't. He could hear her breathing but she didn't say anything. After a few seconds of this, he hung up.

KELLEY PUT ON flip-flops and jogged down the hallway of his apartment building. It smelled like curry and boiling pasta. He didn't know why he was running, or in a hurry, but there was urgency. He'd decided to get drunk. The night was cold but the package store was only half a football field away. He bought a six-pack of tall boys and half a pint of Jim Beam. He didn't usually drink, sometimes sipped a glass or two of wine alongside Rachel, but felt confident this was a solid packy run. He decided on the walk back, his bare arms freezing, clutching the paper bag in his biceps, snug against his chest, that this would be his cleanse.

Kelley couldn't even get through two beers and a swig of the biting Jim Beam before he stopped. He was buzzed and watched the BC Eagles lose to Notre Dame by three touchdowns. After the game, he decided to clean up the apartment, pick himself up. He dumped the dip cups into the toilet and flushed the brown water. He cleaned up the paper plates and iced-coffee cups. He went over to the pizza box but stood over it. He could stomp it and crush the poor mouse. That'd be what Lopez would do, maybe even Rachel. Stomp it to bits. And what Hundley did to that girl. Snipped her apart. How disgusting that was. *I can't even kill a mouse,* he thought. He picked up the box and something slid inside. It may have suffocated and died already, which was a relief. He walked the box over to the door and put it into the hallway. He opened the box and stepped back but nothing ran out. Inside was the half-eaten slice of pizza that he'd used as bait.

———————————

ALL THE SNOW in Barker County melted and Rachel left his life with it. Kelley became OIC of Booking and settled into a routine. He'd read somewhere that routines were perfectly acceptable distractions, if not recommended. One method of this routine became controversial, but when tested, appeared sustainable. He'd decided he would stop calling the inmates by their names, but by their inmate number instead. Initially, identifying a person by a number seemed almost futuristic to him. It felt cold and necessary. He'd thought he'd landed on the perfect balance of making the inmates feel like shit. He wanted them to feel terrible about showing up at his counter. But it was as if they enjoyed returning, coming on the units with their piss-stained bedrolls to high-fives and daps, big appetites for undercooked hard-boiled eggs and stale raisin toast, indigent bags filled with dull razors, a bar of soap, a kid's toothbrush you couldn't grip with more than your thumb and forefinger, shitting and wiping in front of a cellmate, the worst burden, Kelley thought. But there was also a law library with no books, bedbug-ridden cots in the gym when the place filled for the winter, six lockdowns a day, barking COs angry at their hangovers or angry they weren't hungover, AA and NA meeting sign-up sheets posted with no volunteer scheduled to run them. The jail couldn't do more to discourage the men.

One shift, while he was booking in Romano, an old man with skin tags on his neck, arrested without his dentures, who'd done half a dozen rounds with Barker House, Romano asked Kelley if he was of German descent. Romano's empty mouth was disturbing, the absence of something you'd expect to be there but still functional, like a dog with three legs.

"Does Kelley sound German?"

"You call me eleven-oh-seven. Eleven-oh-seven. Eleven-oh-seven. Like I have no name."

"Officer Tully will change you out, eleven-oh-seven."

"Romano. I'm Allen Peter Romano."

"You're eleven-oh-seven again. Welcome back to Barker House."

"Fuck you, I'm Romano. Romano!"

It bothered Kelley, the tie-in to Nazis, so he Googled further into the practice. He found, in fact, the old man was onto something. In the Auschwitz camp, prisoners had serial numbers sewn into their uniforms. Only working prisoners were assigned numbers. Ones who were not were gassed. To Kelley, it seemed in the terrible camp, being assigned a number came with a sense of relief. You were given some reassurance that life was extended, however difficult and inhuman that life would be. Even though assigning a number was dehumanizing and stripped an individual of identity, the SS in fact began the practice *for* identification. Because so many prisoners and soldiers were pouring in, the camps struggled to keep track. By assigning the numbers, the SS was assigning a new identity, not removing one. Also, Dr. House, on the TV show, gave fellowship applicants numbers instead of names. Thirteen was hot. *How'd I forget about* her? he thought.

Other than 1107, the inmates' reactions were muted. Some refused to answer. Some would forget their number and sit in the tank until they were the only one left, thus realizing the last number was their number. The practice quickly deadened any feelings of hope or liveliness from the department. It was as if coming or going, you could cycle through the feelings both would entail.

Tully handed the court list to Kelley. "You hear about Lopez? He's coming back, part time. He's bored at home. Shit, you'll be *his* boss this time."

"Good," Kelley said. "I like Lopez." He checked over his court list and tried not to think about Lopez and stopped at the name *Thaddeus Hundley.*

He was penciled in for returning from court on Kelley's shift. Since Hundley's intake, he'd had hundreds of hours of media coverage: Thaddeus went by Tad; he collected carts at a grocery store; he didn't abuse animals; teachers loved him, and students barely knew him. His great-aunt, toothless and smoking, explained in a rough, rural way that Tad always loved kids and he wouldn't cut the wings off a damn fly. Tad didn't play sports, he had an unknown father, and a boyhood friend saw him break an arm on a rope swing once. In-house the officers noticed that he requested the pod movie on his tier time no matter the genre, liked the bologna at lunch, and was refusing to shave, even on court days.

The bus pulled in and, just as Lopez had before, Kelley cleared the Booking floor. Thaddeus Hundley shuffled into the department through door 1001A, shackled at the hands and feet, guided by two Nashua sheriffs. The bruises on his face were gone, and his eyes had sprung back to their normal openness. He was wearing a white shirt and blue tie with khakis. Court attire. The holding tank stood watchful but they weren't noisy. They were gawking more than contemplating. The shackles were removed, and Kelley walked Tad, Thaddeus, Inmate Hundley, the nephew, the childhood friend, the murderer, Thaddeus Hundley, CCN#56991, to the Property Room by his skinny biceps.

As if by routine, Hundley undressed to nothing and piled his clothes on top of the counter. He was silent and didn't make eye contact with Kelley.

"Those bruises look fresh."

Hundley inspected his stomach. "Ask the morning guy," Hundley said, his voice raw like he hadn't spoken in a long time.

"How you treated on RU?"

"They don't feed me dinner. But I don't eat much." He hid a smile, as if he were fighting off a laugh.

The boy rinsed in the shower with the curtain open. Hundley stepped out, dried off, and Kelley handed him a clean uniform.

"This isn't my uniform."

"I switched it out. It smelled," Kelley said, pushing the orange shirt and pants into Hundley's chest. "They're all the same."

Hundley looked down at the shirt. "The letters are faded on this one. I liked mine, the one with the dark letters."

"You don't own these. You don't own anything. Shut up and get dressed."

Hundley stepped into the pants and pulled them up to his tiny waist, then looked at Kelley. He looked like he'd been crying, not recently, but like all he'd ever done forever was cry. "You hate me, don't you?"

Kelley had to think. He hated what he'd done to the girl. What'd he want him to say? Hundley wanted to be punished. That's it. He enjoyed this.

"Why'd you do it?"

He didn't answer.

"I don't hate you," Kelley said.

Hundley put on his shirt. "You're lying," he said. "Everybody hates me."

"Stop being you, then."

Hundley let out a laugh. "How do I do that?"

"You were assigned a number when you came in," Kelley said. "Be the number."

Hundley seemed to entertain the idea and looked at his green wristband. He mouthed the numbers without saying them. Kelley gave him time to allow the idea to set in. Outside the heavy door, Kelley could hear the beep of the van, the opening of the garage, leg restraints dragging on the floor, the cough of the fat bondsman, a phone ringing, radio bleeps, laughter, and then someone said, "Nah, nah, nah. Not me." Hundley wouldn't look away from his wristband. He might have been waiting for Kelley to sock him, give him a deserved blow. They'd been in the room for enough time for the restraints to be removed and hung up on the wall outside the door. Tully might be out there with his ear pressed to the door, hoping to hear Kelley earn his way. He'd feel some pride for Kelley, for figuring this all out.

He looks around his unit, avoiding the book that's just getting good. He thinks, at night, with all the steel and the ceiling lights off, the darkness lit at eye level by yellow emergency lights only triggered during blackouts or manually by him after lights-out, the unit looks like a slaughterhouse. A perfect place to end a life. The chipped paint and stains on the walls between doors look like scars from hacking tools. Years of old sweat have lacquered the metal beds, cell floors are glossed with urine, scabs and dead skin are embedded in green mattresses, all of which give the unit the decadence of decay. Old, shed animal matter. He hates to think of it this way—a veiled abattoir—but at midnight, without faces in the door windows, the bodies under the wool coverlets could be the bodies of any mammal, the snores could be the snores of fat, resting pigs.

He makes the midnight round in small strides, trying to increase the steps on his pedometer. He's not quite sure how the thing knows how many steps he's taken, or if it's measuring distance. Maybe it's distance; he takes a long stride then two quick short ones, but he forgets the number he started at, so he quits the test. It's old and faulty, so who knows.

He sits back at the table he's settled at for tonight's shift. He picks a different table out of the six each night, so as not to be predictable. During the day, the tables, circled by only nine cells, are excessive. One inmate at a time comes out down here to stretch their legs, forget numbers on the pay phone, wash their balls.

The lazily plotted detective novel he's reading sits on the table in front of him. He's avoided it for the first hour of the shift because Tammy had compiled a package of printouts for his two weeks' vacation in the summer. She tucked them into the book knowing he wouldn't forget it. On his way out the door, while Tammy stared at her enormous phone, her face made up in purple hues, eyelashes wet and curled, but her mouth cleaned of pink lipstick, she directed him to "choose a place we can tolerate for seven days." She said "tolerate" slowly, as if telling him she knew this would be hard for him to do but *please, Tony, think this through. Imagine yourself, along with me, your wife, the one who has carefully chosen these four places—Tony, you pick one, it's not that hard—where we can fill our days with activities, tours, things you want to do, don't just think of me.*

He makes his rounds clockwise during even hours, counter-clockwise during odd, counting his steps at Tammy's suggestion. In some queer ritual to the jail gods, he's done it this way every night since he came to third shift, after his eleventh year on the job, when a biker from Mason—wanting to make a name before going upstate—cut Tony's neck with a shaving razor jammed into a toothbrush.

Prior to the assault, Tony had been working U4 for a few months, not making enemies, but not making friends either. He coasted, forged D-tickets, searched cells with more interest in what the inmates inside were reading than hiding. Earned a paycheck, kept his head down, and allowed Ashley the privilege of good schooling. He was seated on a stool inside a cell flipping through *Gerald's Game*, he remembers, because who can forget that opening scene, the handcuffs and heart attack. Poor Gerald. The large, hairy inmate ran up on Tony. Quickly he sliced Tony's neck—the efficiency later made Tony think it'd been planned for a while—and then left the cell. The blood scared Tony. There was too much of it. But after his radio call, during the silence that followed, Tony didn't think of Tammy or Ashley. He thought of the scuff marks on the ceiling, from sneakers, and how they got there.

Luckily for Tony, the inmate only wanted to assault an officer, not kill one, and the cut wasn't deep enough to end it all.

The Josephses were scheduled to vacation at Old Orchard Beach, a trailer rental, with paddleboats and horseshoes. But the injury forced Tammy to cancel the trip. And now it's

January, the month when the officers are expected to hand in their vacation request forms for the year. Most officers choose the same days every year: two weeks in the summer, Thanksgiving, and the week of Christmas and New Year's. Tony's eighteen-year seniority ensures his request never gets denied. His first few years on the job he'd slept through Christmas morning because he couldn't get the eve off. She'd had to wait until lunch to open her presents. Having not done any of the shopping, he was just as surprised as Ashley was opening her gifts, just not as excited. An Easy-Bake oven. A doll that drank from a bottle and even shat itself. He tried to make the best of the situation for Ashley, but she blamed him, of course, because what child could understand responsibility?

Vacations were a front, a way for Tammy to pretend they were a family. Since Tony had worked second shift for the majority of Ashley's childhood, he rarely saw them. She'd go to St. Anne's on Farragut Street in Hudson, now a crumbling brick building with high, waving flags, military housing for disabled vets. Then he'd sleep. He'd be off to the jail before she got out of school and he wouldn't see her or Tammy. Pre-cell-phone, check-ins were notes left by Tammy for him to read when he woke up in the late afternoon. *Ashley lost another tooth* or *The movie rentals are due today*. His two-week vacation was his time to be a parent to Ashley. First, in her early years while at the deplorably majestic Magic Kingdom, as Daddy. Then, in the preteen years, traversing the Franconia Range, burning his calves on the rugged trails, not concerned with fun but completion, he was Dad. He can't remember when he became just

Tony to Ashley. Maybe it was after Montreal, where he snuck out buzzed one poorly planned night, down cold St. Catherine's Street in a T-shirt. While Tammy and Ashley slept, he stumbled under neon French signs, boring English signs. The smell of seared gyro meat on street corners tempted him. He climbed two flights of dark stairs and perched at the stage, let strippers pull dollar coins from his teeth with their ass cheeks. He returned to the hotel as the sun rose and slept the entire last day away while the girls toured. Anyway, it happened, and the only one to fight her on using his given name was Tammy.

Tammy is clinging to some old ideas, family time, and she is misguided. Tony doesn't look at the vacation package. He reads forty-something pages of the paperback and logs 641 steps on his pedometer. Reading began as an escape. It started after high school, all those years ago, in a rebellion against his father's pleadings for him to join the service. Tony attended a community college where he intended to study nothing, just continue his life as he knew it: chasing tail and reading about narrators chasing tail. Wanderers on the road were heroes. Sal and Dean. But he became enamored with a literature professor, a short, astute man, who always had crust on the corners of his mouth, who pegged Tony as exactly who he was. The teacher impressed other writings on Tony, classics; Tony fell in love with the Wife of Bath and Lord Walter's wife, women who treated men like women. He wanted a woman who could strangle his soul. He lurked about the feminist circles; they were big then, the circles, raw and real, not like now. It seems to Tony that the feminist circles are hiding now. It's a shame, because they were good places to find women. It was there he found Tammy. Some time ago, he stumbled across that professor in a smut shop, thumbing through a titty mag, but the man didn't recognize him.

TONY'S LUNCH BREAK is at 0130 hours. Mitchell relieved him from RU and he is now fishing through the tremendous amount of Tupperware in the large staff lounge refrigerator. He finds it where he definitely didn't leave it. Nielsen and Jeffries sit together at a round table, and Nielsen is reading a stapled printout. The *Barker House Gazette*. For the past few years an unknown third shifter—Tony presumes third shift but because the author is unknown he can't say for certain, though it always appears on third shift—has created a monthly issue of the newspaper. The first Monday of every month, the paper is scattered around the locker room, muster room, and staff lounge and can be read until about nine o'clock when the captain comes in and rounds up all the copies and shreds them. It is filled with insults and jokes, some fictional, some based in fact. The author doesn't shy from anyone, which is why the captain is red-assed about it. Tony wishes he had the gall to produce such a thing. But he always makes his rounds, shines a light on the numbered bodies, punches out when his paperwork is cleared. Besides, who has the time?

Nielsen laughs and Jeffries eats the last lumps of flesh from an apple. They're the only other two on break and usually eat together each night, the three of them being the only second-floor officers. Tammy packed his lunch: turkey meat-balls on a bed of spaghetti squash. *We can't have your heart going again, Tony. You'll never know the difference with the squash. Christ, Tony, if you have to, close your damn eyes when you eat it.*

Tony suspects Jeffries is the producer of the gazette. He rarely appears interested in the paper or laughs at some of the outlandish front pages. Tony has never made the acclaimed front page, him not having risen to the well-known status most front-pagers have. He wonders if the gazette had been around when he had his neck slit if he would've made the front page then.

Jeffries gets up and walks over to the candy machine. Jeffries cuts his own hair, brags about the money he saves, but he never seems to get his clipper far enough into the roll of fat on the back of his head, so the hair is longer there, and darker. This bothers Tony but he doesn't point it out to Jeffries.

Jeffries comes back with a Whatchamacallit and Nielsen cracks a hard-boiled egg on a napkin and starts to peel off the shell. He nods at Tony, his eyes wide behind his thin glasses.

"What the hell are you eating?" Nielsen asks. His neck is lined with red pimples where it rubs against the collar.

"Meatballs and fake spaghetti," Tony says and cuts a meat-ball with the side of his spork. "The wife."

"Rough," Jeffries says as he opens the candy bar wrapper with his teeth. "I'm never getting married. I don't see the appeal."

Tony can't agree more. In fact, he tells Jeffries that, who then tilts his candy bar at Tony.

"Why'd you get hitched?" Jeffries asks, chocolate smeared on his front teeth.

"I got suckered in," Tony says.

Which is true. Tony never intended to get married. It happened from working with older guys. Before the jail, he detailed boats in Winnipesaukee, enjoyed the banter, the sun, the way he could hang off a bowrider with one hand and work the heavy buffer with the other, the drinks cool in his worn hand after hard labor while the sun went into the lake. The crew were all married, with Little League games and wrestling meets. Tony romanticized this future. He never went back to school after community college. Instead he buffed enough boats to pay rent on their place so Tammy could finish school. They always agreed he'd go back, but then she got pregnant with Ashley. Tammy let him down. She abandoned a sexy social cause for a safe job on campus. It was all short hair and padded bras after that. Before Ashley, they used to shower together, mess around. They talked about books. She cared about her figure and drank Slimfasts. She let him drink his Sundays away during football season. After Ashley's birth, none of that. There's no point in kicking himself, he thinks. Everything he ever imagines to be in the future is different when he gets there. It won't be any different for Jeffries, whatever path he thinks best.

A cartoon of two officers having sex with a woman is on the back page of the gazette. Tony eats a meatball and stares at it. The officer in her mouth is disheveled, his hair messy, his stomach fat. The officer in the rear wears a cowboy hat, and the two men are double-high-fiving above the woman. Nielsen sees

Tony looking at the cartoon and folds the paper back to see what he's looking at.

"That's called an Eiffel Tower," Nielsen says.

Goddamn cartoons now. Tony thinks about what goes into publishing the paper, the lengths the author goes to. He—maybe it's a she; he hasn't considered that—puts a good deal of work into the gazette and for zero notoriety. A present-day Thomas Paine minus the need for an overthrow or a sense of urgency. He feels his comparison is a bit inadequate or rushed and then thinks the gazette is more *Modest Proposal* with the *Common Sense* anonymity. Too archaic to share. Too elitist. *You're a dirty guard, Tony; don't go pretending you're not.* Plus, that doesn't work because the headline he sees in front of him, "Nude photos surface proving Karl's dick *is* a black mamba," is more parody than satire and he begins to question his comparisons. It hits him. It's like *MAD Magazine. That was right in front of your face, Tony.*

"You guys ever do an Eiffel Tower?" Tony asks.

"I was in a frat," Nielsen says.

Nielsen picks the paper back up. Ice cubes drop and clunk in the ice machine behind Tony. Jeffries chews the candy bar with his mouth open, probably intentionally, not because of a cold. Outside, it is frigid and dark, the city surrounding the jail awake and mischievous, hookers pulling in johns to pay for heroin, junkies breaking into homes for valuables to pawn at King's in the morning, only to have the transactions and receipts handed over to police soon after. Those awake this time of night, half lit on God knows what, would all make a trip through the House sooner or later. Tony knows all this without needing a window.

This is why he reads those dumb paperbacks he buys at CVS when he picks up his anticoagulants. He gets in a mood where all things are shitty. Henna—yes, Henna—his perky thirty-two-year-old psychologist, with her tight bun, the incense-smelling office on the third floor where the floors squeak oddly loud, suggested he tone down his reading material. Reading about Attila the Hun's death march or rereading *Crime and Punishment* for the third time because he remembers a part where Dostoyevsky reveals himself in the text as the narrator—he can't remember where or how but he knows he saw it once—he told Henna all this and then some, and she calmly told Tony maybe to not read those books, especially during work hours (he told her about the slaughterhouse feel of the unit, too). After the heart attack, which Tammy attributed to stress, mainly from Ashley bolting—*because your diet is impeccable, Tony, unless you're not eating what I send with you, but that fatty jail food, and I know you're not eating that, are you, Tony?*—she insisted Tony needed to work through things. Hence, Henna. Now he misses his books, the hidden enrichment. He misses when things mattered at all.

"The thing about Eiffel Towers," Nielsen begins, "is that the formation is only a snapshot of what is going on. It's a quick high-five. You know, you don't actually stay that way."

Nielsen is the youngest of the three, big-chested, but with a delicate face. He's on third shift because he watches his kid while his wife works during the day. It's sad to watch a guy turn nocturnal for a baby. *Actually, maybe it isn't,* Tony thinks. Maybe if he'd spent more time with Ashley as a baby, she wouldn't have turned out the way she did. *Don't go second-guessing yourself, Tony. It's not in your makeup.* But Henna might piggyback that idea, so he mentally notes it for their next session.

———————————

HE DOESN'T TELL his wife he didn't even so much as glance at her vacation package. She leaves for work at the school when he walks in the house at seven thirty. She works in financial aid, has for twenty years, marked last year by a plaque the university gave her that she hung above the kitchen table like it was a trophy. Big fucking deal. Thanks for doing the basic task we ask of you: show up. He earns colored ribbons from accolades unknown to Tammy; she doesn't even pretend to care and he's never found reason to boast. He wears them every day. What if he had pointed them out to Ashley when she was younger? "The yellow one is for the time I blew life into someone who didn't want it anymore." Would that have kept her? Was he even why she left, or was she always going to leave? Were they all going to be where they are now, no matter what? If that lowlife had actually died that sweaty afternoon, if Tony's breath had proved unsuccessful—his chest pumps, his silent pleadings for the man he didn't know—would it all be the same? Tammy kisses him on the cheek—she hates his mustache—and goes out the door smiling, smelling like blueberry streusel.

Once she's backed out and is down the street a bit, he walks out to his car in his slippers, his feet cold and crunching the week-old snow, and grabs the grocery bag from the trunk. He empties the contents—he does this every work morning—onto the counter: a thirteen-ounce Delmonico steak, pre-packaged potato salad, and two Budweisers. Tammy would be surprised to see him cook, to see him work the smoking pan, season the meat with equal parts sea salt, pepper, and garlic powder, lay the meat down for a two-minute sear, then slather a spoonful of butter on after a turn and kick it into the oven to finish it off. Perfectly pink. It's nothing special. Maybe he'd show her one day, as if he's learned simple guitar chords in secret and is going to surprise her with "Love Me Do."

After he's full, he smokes a Parliament while sitting on the toilet, blowing smoke out of the bathroom window. The cool air comes in and collides with the hot steam from the shower and the cigarette smoke. This is the best part of his day. The clandestine silence and solitude. He drops the cigarette between his legs and he sits there for a while. He thinks of Ashley and it ruins his mood. He concludes she is a runner. Henna has been on him to call her. Call her, he thinks, to find out what he already knows. Ashley is twenty-one and moved to San Diego when she turned eighteen. Not married but has a son, contemporary arrangements. She's a barista, minimum wage plus tips. His only grandchild—grandson even—has hair longer than a girl's. He's three, his name is Ethan, and in the only photo he has of Ethan the boy is wearing a Nirvana

T-shirt, some yellow smiley face. It's a band, Tammy says. *Remember Kurt Cobain?* No, he doesn't. What three-year-old knows what bands he likes? Ashley wouldn't talk to him anyway even if he did call. *I get too upset,* she says. *You don't listen. You're too uptight.* And maybe he is. If she did try to reach out to him she would see he's much better now. The heart attack put things in perspective. He's much more civil with Tammy. They're planning a vacation. He suspects Ashley calls her mother during the day. They talk about him and enjoy their complicity.

He won't call. He showers and sleeps heavily all day.

WORKING THIRD SHIFT, he enjoys three dinners a day. He's fine with that. He was never a fan of breakfast food. But his wife makes him quinoa and buckwheat now since his heart attack. He understands her reasoning and he doesn't have the energy to fight her on it. It hasn't helped her avocado frame. He wakes up at five twenty and they eat chicken hot dogs and bean salad and he doesn't hate it. She wears a red Mickey Mouse T-shirt, white-and-black-checkered pajama pants, thick ashy eye makeup, her around-the-house attire. She cuts her hot dog into tiny pieces, slivers, and then chews them like a monster. He eats quickly. They talk some; his wife asks him how he feels, if he's tired, he should take it easy, but he couldn't take it much easier. She waits until he's almost done eating and she asks about the vacation, *you know, Tony, where is it you think you're leaning toward*, and he says the resort, most likely, and he's pleased with himself because she's leaning that way too.

————————————

IN THE BOOK he's reading, the detective's daughter is trying to sabotage the investigation. Obviously this makes him think of Ashley again. If only she knew how much he thought of her. It may be because this chapter of his life is currently being dissected by Henna, but he wouldn't tell Ashley that if they got to talking. He's aggravated he has to reread the last few pages, having been sidetracked. The detective, the hero, knows what his daughter is doing but allows her to continue—this is some-thing she needs—while trying to solve the case. He looks for the author picture but the book doesn't have one. The narrative doesn't hold a spine to the mere description of a typhoon attacking the *Pequod*, or Benjy's squeal at soiled drawers, or even an inventive portrait of Anna.

He makes an even round. All the inmates are asleep and snoring. It's early in the shift and Tony is well rested, but he gets tired watching them sleep. The inmates look comfortable, dreaming, and for the eight to ten hours of sleep they are playing with their kids, catching footballs, snorting coke, and licking women. To Tony, the inmates during third shift are not the same during the day shifts. He doesn't hate them or feel sorry for them at night.

Tony sits back down and handwrites the round onto his log: *2330 Round Made.* The pedometer is stuck on 999. He flips the lever and it resets, settles back at 999. He pockets it. The vacation package is underneath the clipboard. He eyes it for a moment. He knows he'll have to soon but he's tired. He gives up on the novel and thumbs through the gazette he'd swiped from the lounge, figures he could use a laugh. But he finds himself fixated on the cartoon of the two officers in uniform tag-teaming who he decides to be Tully's wife, a first shifter who, rumor has it, works overtime so his wife can screw around with some cowboy from Texas, hence the cowboy hat. Tony doesn't get involved with rumors but he lets himself on this one, giving context to the cartoon, adding much-needed layers. The gazette artist doesn't draw as well as he writes.

Tony gets hard, not intentionally, just one of those times when something unknown takes the controls. He can feel his heart thumping and it worries him. *Tony, relax. Remember what Dr. Almonte said, Tony, your heart can't play like it used to. Take some deep breaths and act like you care when you do it.* He folds up the gazette and hides it along with the vacation papers and then picks the paperback up and reads.

He thinks about the last time Tammy felt real. He settles on the day after Ashley left, leaving only an Internet message. Tammy blamed him. She stood over her laptop, in a loose brown blouse and orange slacks that hid her rounding ass, and she read over and over *I'm gone. I'm never coming back* to Tony. And Tony leaned against the kitchen counter, his hands in his pockets, the coffee maker spitting the last drops from the reservoir, and stared at the free calendar from their car insurance company on the wall, the slick teal Jaguar for June, and wanted to call Ashley's bluff for the hundredth time but it felt genuine this time, the pregnancy, the bomb. When Tony wouldn't speak, wouldn't take his eyes off that beautiful car, Tammy pulled his hair and screamed and it took him two weeks to speak to her but maybe he never really spoke to her again.

He's still hard and he rubs himself. He wants to de-fat Tammy, to strip her of domesticity and care and elongate her shriveled, graying hair. He imagines her ball-gagged, in a wedding dress, crawling around their living room rug on a leash. One breast is hanging out of the dress, flopping around. She is slim and young, like when they met. She wears bright makeup and black lipstick. Holding the end of the leash is a naked man. Another man stands behind his wife, stroking his dick. Tony is there, too, but in his uniform sitting on the couch. He wants to watch. The two men are Nielsen and Jeffries. The one with his back to Tony, stroking his dick, is Jeffries because of the back of his head. Maybe Tony's part in the scenario is jamming clippers into the roll and evening it out finally. Nielsen tugs at the leash and barks like a dog. Soon, the wedding dress is pulled off and the ball gag taken out and it's as if no one knows or cares he is there. The two men and his wife fuck on the floor.

He replays this over and over in his head, his penis pulsating through his thin pants. It's come out of the slit in his boxers. He hurries over to the storage closet and stands over the floor sink, beginning to masturbate. Quickly, as if the semen had been waiting at the tip, he comes into the drain. Another first for work.

The excitement is expelled down the drain. In its place, he feels jealous of the men. He makes a round. He looks in each cell and wonders if someone had seen him or pieced together what just happened, but they all look like they've been asleep for a while.

He'd never fantasized about Tammy before. She looked loose and athletic, like she wanted what was happening. They're both forty-six and sex shouldn't be dead for them but it is. *Your heart, Tony,* she'd say, *you can't die on top of me.* But now, Tony wonders if he'd missed something. The way she bounced on Jeffries's (or was it Nielsen's?) dick, squatting like a catcher, well, she'd never done that with Tony. And anal. Both men almost got inside her at once. How come he never ventured back there? He starts to feel hard again so he makes an unscheduled round.

"WHAT'S ON THE menu tonight, chief?" Nielsen asks, rolling an egg, gently cracking it, ensuring the inside stayed intact.

Tony looks in his Tupperware that he's yet to heat. Vegan carbonara. White noodles, dirt-colored mushrooms, and a sprinkle of withered peas.

"I don't think I'm going to eat this," Tony says. "I don't think I can do a round two."

"I just submitted my vacay request form," Nielsen says. "Beach house. Hampton in August."

"You enjoy that," Tony says and puts the lid back on the Tupperware.

Jeffries laughs at a video on his phone. Tony can't guess now who is behind the gazette. *You just have to let these things go,*

Tony. What are you going to do, alienate yourself from everyone your whole life? But he just wants to shake the author's hand.

"Hey," Nielsen says, "you going to toss that? Emily has been up and down with Nora and she hasn't made me a dinner in weeks. I'll take some home loving off your hands."

Tony slides the food to Nielsen. "It'll just go to waste."

Nielsen eats the food cold. Beach house. Poor bastard. The kid will fry. Oh, vacations—he wants to orate to Nielsen—at their core, are getaways from reality. But really, what is a vacation? It's a tease, that's what it is. You get to see how others live. The well-off, the ones lucky enough to be born on a tropical island. All it does is show you an existence out of your reach. He remembers a local man on the beach at St. Thomas recently, carving faces into coconuts. Happy as shit. And the owner of the sailboat that took them from one Carolina to the other, drinking wine the entire time, wearing fabric Tony'd never seen before. Dick. Nothing about him felt real.

"The beach," Tony says. "You guys will love that."

HE'S GETTING TO the end of the detective novel. The hero has solved the case but doesn't know if he can forgive his daughter. He thinks he can't but when he goes to her apartment and she opens the door, he is filled with relief and love and all is forgiven. Cheesy fucking ending. What happened to betrayal? Or betrayal seeded in love. Lenny, you're not for this world, Lenny. *But, Tony, you have to think of the audience. Women*

might like quiet endings. It's always about what you want, Tony,
but the world isn't yours.

He gets that, and that's why he isn't irate with the ending,
just not happy with it. He makes a round but stops halfway. He
feels a pain in his chest and panics. He swallows a few times but
his mouth still fills with saliva. He braces himself on a cell door.
The door is cold and feels good on his forehead. He traces a
long scratch on the door with his finger, up and down, up and
down. The pain subsides and he arches his back, stretches his
chest, and finishes the round.

He picks up the clipboard and looks at the vacation pack-
ages: Napa Valley, Grand Canyon, Key West, and Virginia Beach.
He wants to sigh but no one would hear. He wants someone to
complain to but everyone's asleep. He gets a pain in his chest
again but doesn't panic. When it leaves, he puts the package
back under the clipboard.

This odd young officer, Mankins, who, first thing each
morning, opens the rec yard door to let the cold air in, relieves
him. He gets why he does it, Mankins's way of terrorizing the
inmates. It's only caused a ruckus once so far, but it'll happen
again. Tony figures he'll let Mankins learn the hard way. All it
takes is a shiv to the jugular to change your thinking.

He punches out without talking to any of the other officers
and leaves the building. The morning sky is becoming bright,
the air chilly. He sucks it in, lights a cigarette, and thinks about
how many mornings he has left. *Don't condemn yourself,* Henna
would say. *If you're going to be like that, Tony, then what's the*

point of it all? He feels the three-inch scar on his neck, but it's almost flush with the rest of his skin now. Ashley is an early riser, he knows, because she opens the coffee shop six days a week. She'd be up, he thinks, for sure. Or, maybe with the time difference, it's too early. Could be. He watches the sun rise over Barker House, Lt. Hobson raise the flag and salute it, the highway crew pile into the county vans, the new academy cadets jog laps around the parking lot, and smokes three more cigarettes. There's one left in the pack and he lights it. He decides to try Ashley.

He pulls his flip phone—the one he swore he'd only use for emergencies—out of the glove box. After plugging it into the light outlet, then turning it on, he calls the only number he has of Ashley's. Tammy had programmed it in shortly after the heart attack. *Make amends, Tony, if not for Ashley, for Ethan.* It rings for a while and Ashley answers.

"Hi," he says, his voice surprising him. "It's me. Tony."

There is silence. And then, "What do you want, Tony?"

Tony can hear a child's voice in the background, a loud TV. He takes a drag of the cigarette. "Is that him?" he asks. "Is that my grandson?"

"Put it down," she says, but not to Tony. "I'm busy."

And then he hears, "Who's Tony?" He hears it in his blood, his soul.

"Can I talk to the little man?"

"He doesn't know you."

Tony stares at the passenger seat in his truck, tries to remember Ashley there, a father-daughter ride they shared, a memory to rattle her, but can't. He wants to tell her there was no other way. Once he sought this route it was his to finish. Life doesn't have to be traumatizing or insulting. *For God's sake, Ashley, you had it damn good compared to most.* Instead, he sees the vacation papers.

"Your mother and I were thinking of vacationing out there," he says. "Near you."

"Don't."

He hears the small voice ask again who Tony is before there's no one on the line. He holds the phone to his ear. "Ethan," he says.

Tony flings the phone into the glove box and slams it shut. As the sun rises behind the jail, as the air from the truck's vents turn from cold to warm, Tony closes his eyes. He shuffles the printouts and lays them on the passenger seat. At random, he points to their next vacation destination.

Part IV

UNDERHAND

J ust get over here," Tully says over his shoulder, as if O'Brien were right behind him. He yells into the speakerphone and his free hands grip the bat. O'Brien doesn't answer and Tully takes a healthy hack in the center of the garage. He collects himself. "I have beers."

"No getting weird," O'Brien says. "Big day tomorrow."

Tully twists his palms over the rubbery handle. "We'll do what we gotta do."

Tully rarely visits the garage. It doesn't have many tools. It holds just lacrosse sticks, a cobwebby three-piece luggage set missing the carry-on, bags of bark mulch, and kids' bicycles. Tully's kids have outgrown them but his nostalgia for the two-wheelers outweigh his need for free space. The garage smells distinctly of motor oil, caused by a spilt bottle of Pennzoil behind the sagging boxes of Christmas lights in the rear of the garage, the lights similar to the Pennzoil and filter purchase made by Tully. He's a father, a homeowner, yet the things he imagines he is supposed to enjoy are only enjoyable in the conceptual stage. The lawn gets cut and the leaves raked, the roof doesn't leak. Anything beyond is, well, beyond. He does enjoy the manly smell of the oil, and since he can't necessarily see the spill, he doesn't feel the need to clean it.

As he waits for O'Brien, he heads up the wooden steps and into the house. He takes a beer from the fridge and drinks half of it in the quiet kitchen. Outside, it is windy and cold, but not yet pitch-black. The autumn moon is fat and white, giving off a hazy light through the window over the sink. Tully hasn't eaten all day. He searches the fridge and finds a bagged-up rotisserie chicken he's already picked the skin off. As he eats the rest with his fingers in between sips of beer, he feels O'Brien come into the kitchen behind him. It's a skill he picked up at the House. Never have your back to a doorway. If you do, learn to feel when someone is behind you. He continues to eat as he stands at the island.

"Turn a light on," O'Brien says. "You depress the shit out of me." Tully squeezes his eyes shut when O'Brien flicks on the ceiling fan light above him. He blinks and chews.

"You bring the attachment?"

"It's a cylinder hone," O'Brien answers, feeling knowledge-able. "And yes, I brought it." O'Brien puts the metal tool on the island. "You talk to Kathy at all lately?"

He wipes his greasy cheek on his shoulder, then touches it with his dry hand to inspect for food juice. There isn't any. "Pierce is in the garage. Grab a beer." Tully cleans his oily hands on his sweatpants and heads for the garage. "Grab a few," he says, and turns the light off on the way out of the kitchen.

In the garage, O'Brien tries the light. It doesn't work. He's concerned for Tully but tries not to be because Tully wears on him. Tully can sulk all he wants but it's his own fault. Kathy—who, O'Brien always thought, is a great woman—left him and is not going to return. But Tully used to give him rides to work after his DUI. He'd headed to Murphy's Taproom after work and hit dollar draft night hard. It was an icy night and O'Brien drove home. A college kid in a beat-up Taurus slid into O'Brien at a red light. Damage was minimal, but the kid insisted on calling the police. It wasn't uncommon to carry a DUI or two at the House, as long as you didn't get the third one. Since the gossipy rides, Tully has invited him to his kid's birthday parties and cookouts. It is a forced friendship, one that O'Brien feels is on its last legs.

They both still play in the Fallen Officers annual softball tournament. Had that not been the case, O'Brien wouldn't be here, trailing Tully into his depression den of a garage. Captain Dixon would reach out to them both, cordially, as if they'd left the House on good terms. But they are the two best hitters, and Tully plays a mean shortstop—a difficult position to lock down on ragtag softball squads. And this year has a different meaning: the Barker House squad is playing in honor of Eric Menser, a sad sack O'Brien had a soft spot for, who, one night, dressed in his pressed uniform, drove out to a Gold's Gym parking lot in the wee morning hours and shot himself through his mouth. No one has ever been killed while working at the House. But they've had plenty of officers kill themselves. Menser hit them softer than when Sam Knudsen offed himself. No one could pinpoint a reason why Sam would do it.

O'Brien sits on the garage steps and sips his beer while Tully stands on a milk crate and changes the bulb. The garage is colder than the outside, enough so O'Brien regrets wearing gym shorts. Tully switches his attention to the bat, Pierce Brosnan. Tully slides his hand up the barrel and cups the top and tries to twist the end cap off like opening a beer bottle.

"You can't get it off like that."

"I feel it moving," Tully says. He has thick forearms, as, O'Brien thinks, a laborer should. Tully lugs bricks and rocks now. O'Brien also has a more suitable job since he left the House. He began substituting and went back to school, studying math. And this past semester, he landed a long-term sub position. O'Brien won't tell Tully about his job at the school, because doing that would mean he might accidentally summon thoughts of Keely, the seventeen-year-old junior on whom he has a grotesquely boyish crush. Even now, he's thinking of her smooth, round face, her volleyball thighs, and the mysterious flower she smells like each day. It kills O'Brien, in a way he's not proud of, not knowing what that flower is. Some days when school lets out he goes to Walmart and smell-tests body sprays and hand lotions, tells the clerk he's browsing for the wife he doesn't have. Vanilla Orchid, Cherry Blossom, Cucumber Melon, White Musk. Closest he's come is a hand cream named Pacific Ocean, which makes no fucking sense. But it smells like a counterfeit flower, a synthetic jasmine that bears no resemblance to its natural scent, just a familiar name to put on the bottle. Even so, he now drinks jasmine tea at night, tells himself it isn't lust for Keely, he just wants to fall asleep with his face in her hair, his chin against her soft neck.

"You really want to ruin Pierce?" O'Brien asks. At last year's tournament, Markowski mistakenly gave the bat the Irish actor's name after he deemed the bat of French descent. The bat has a blue, white, and red pattern, in that order, and Markowski's best defense was "Isn't Pierce a French name, assholes?"

"We can always buy a new bat."

Tully continues to try and pry the cap off with his bare hands. The garage is too quiet for O'Brien. Keely's essence follows him, lingers in his throat as if he'd walked through her delicate mist. O'Brien swishes the beer in his mouth in an attempt to quell the phantom taste of jasmine. He feels embarrassed about the constant thinking of Keely. She has a dark freckle on the left side of her neck, just under her jawline. Her hair is so blonde he thinks it's colored, but he's never seen dark roots. She squints to see the whiteboard. She rides horses. He feels Keely is the most American girl he's ever met.

He needs a moment alone. O'Brien goes inside the house and into the kitchen that smells of pasta sauce and greasy chicken. The kitchen is clean, the centered island free of clutter, the refrigerator free of magnets and obituaries and children's sports schedules. The only light on is the one above the sink that barely reaches the far end of the kitchen. O'Brien finds the pots and pans cabinet, pulls out a speckled lobster pot, fills it halfway with water in the sink, and puts it on the stove.

Just before it comes to a boil, O'Brien carries the pot cautiously into the garage. Steam from the boiling water hits his face and he can feel the moisture collect in his beard. Tully is on a little girl's bike, stroking the rainbow-colored streamers that dangle from the tiny handlebars. O'Brien wonders if he is inspecting it for defects. But he seems to just be sitting on it. O'Brien sets the pot down in the center of the cement floor.

"Dunk Pierce in this for a minute."

Tully, still on the bike and holding the bat, rolls across the garage. Without hesitation, he sticks the barrel into the hot water. They both stare into the pot as if the water were capable of transforming the bat, as if it were some property-enhancing cauldron in which Pierce will emerge magically infused. But they aren't trying to enhance it through addition; they are taking away a part of it to make Pierce dangerously effective.

"That's long enough," O'Brien says, as if he were some authority on appropriate heat. Tully listens and out comes the glistening wet bat. There are tiny strings of steam dancing off the barrel in the garage's white light. Tully slides the bat through the handlebars of the girl's bike, secures the knob end between his knees, and easily pops the cap off with a flathead. O'Brien leans in to inspect the end of the bat for scuff marks, anything an ump or opposing player could see to accuse them of doctoring it. But he also wants to get a look inside the bat. Their foreheads nearly touch as they peer into the business end of Pierce.

"Doesn't look like much," O'Brien says.

"What the hell were you expecting?"

"It's a three-hundred-dollar bat."

"Get the thing."

"It's a cylinder hone."

Tully ditches the bike against some luggage. He stands in the center of the now humid garage, the pot of water evaporating in the closed-off space. Tully puts the knob end between his knees again and double-fists the barrel tightly.

"Feed her in."

O'Brien puts the attachment on the power drill he brought. He had remembered to juice the battery before he left for school so he could be in and out, get this over with. Tully could make any night an all-nighter, maybe try to talk O'Brien into sneaking off to Peddler's Daughter or the Garden. He is a dog. They'd gone out for beers a few times in the last year or so but Tully always took the night too far, wanting to linger in the bar until the women loosened. *Piggies*, he called them. He ran around on Kathy and wasn't shy about it, even had a short fling with CO Brenner. After a few rounds, Tully was apt to go to the bathroom and come out wedding-ring-less. But if he'd struck out, he'd start talking about Brenner. She was much younger and O'Brien thought maybe he could bring up Keely; he so wants to confess to someone about his thoughts of her, but he hasn't yet.

The cylinder hone looks like a grappling hook with a foot-long hose. As O'Brien feeds it into the bat, the tool compresses.

"I got her," Tully says, and O'Brien starts the drill. The hone screeches inside Pierce. The sound reminds O'Brien of the trade high school, the hallway of shops in the old building.

Tully holds the bat and watches the barrel for any bubble spots. He knows what they are doing is wrong, but there is no way they can win the tournament, not with the squad they have. They are annual one-and-dones. Cheating at men's softball.

"I thought, when I was a kid, being an adult would be all motorboating and baking cakes," Tully says over the grinding metal.

"Strange sentiment."

"I remember it. The day I had that thought. A snow day, and my brother was watching squiggle porn on the TV. I thought all I'd ever do was put my mouth in between giant boobs and buy cake mix and frosting and just live. Kiss boobs. All day."

"And bake cakes."

"Every kind of cake I could get my hands on."

Over the grinding metal, O'Brien says, "You ever think about Menser?"

"I guess. Once in a while."

"I sometimes wonder what the last thing he thought was."

"He never got all mushy with me. I knew the kid had problems, but to eat his gun. Shit."

"Maybe if he didn't bottle it all up and got mushy once in a while he wouldn't have made the decision he did."

"He made a dumb decision to leave this world."

"There's an argument in defense of leaving."

"I don't agree with that," Tully says. "I've been through some shit. Much worse than Menser. It's a bitch move."

"There's courage in pulling the trigger."

Tully's grip loosens.

"Hold it steady," O'Brien says. Last year, the House lost to a team of public defenders. The year before, they got so drunk, Pelham PD mercy-ruled them in the fourth inning. But this year they are playing for the big guy. Bring home the trophy so the superintendent can display it in his office. O'Brien stares at the spinning drill and can smell the grinding metal. He thinks he'd shaved enough of the inner barrel, but keeps the drill running in hopes of bubbling the exterior, making the bat unusable. He can be a silent hero in this moment. He even congratulates himself for coming up with the idea on the fly. But Tully intervenes.

"Cut her off," Tully says. "Do it now!"

O'Brien turns the drill off and slides out the hone. Tully turns the bat over, checking the barrel, and then both men peer again inside.

"I think we have a chance this year," Tully says. He hands Pierce to O'Brien, then goes and sits down on Erin's bike. He picks his beer off the shelf. He imagines hitting a ball over the left field fence and slowly trotting around the bases. He smiles at the image of himself stomping on home plate and high-fiving his old workmates. He wonders if Brenner will come watch this year. He hasn't seen her since his last shift. She wouldn't talk to him. He'd been advised to resign by the superintendent on account of his vehicular misdeeds, so there was no cake or balloons. He just punched out, dropped his two sets of uniforms off to Hobson, and left the House for the last time. He'd stood in the parking lot and drunk beers with Lopez and Kelley, told jokes from the House, particular inmates who were wronged in humorous ways. The skinner they used to feed toilet bowl sand-wiches. The Indian guy they had convinced that he had just awoken from a years-long coma. That stuff could make the job fun.

SHE LAYS OUT her uniform and the butterflies start. She'd heard Lt. Hobson say a few ex-screws were coming back to play, ones that had worked closely with Menser. Everyone at the House is close, tough not to be, with all the shit you go through together. But when you partner up with someone for months, there's an intimate relationship, you know their mood without asking, know if something's going on at home, can tell if they are wearing the same uniform as they had yesterday by the pattern of sweat stains. And many of the old-timers had that relationship with Menser, though mostly fraught; he was still capable of eliciting the rare feeling of sympathy. He was abra-sive and a crap officer, overweight, took care of his aphasic mother who suffered a stroke after her husband died suddenly. Whenever he was mandated to stay another shift, he'd throw a tantrum, punch lockers; once he ripped up his ID card. There was a rumor he brought in a doctor's note to the lieutenant saying he couldn't work overtime. Brenner thinks she was easy on him but can't remember. She was, at the time, having a quasi-affair with Tully, the Property officer. But she didn't know he was married. Or did she? Yes, she did.

When she heard of the tournament, no one invited her or any other women officers to play. The only other women officers are Goggin and Pratt, second shifters, both of who are heavyset lesbians who married last year. They plan on buying an alpaca farm in Marlboro with their retirement.

A week before the day of the tourney, in the tiny muster room before shift, which smelled like aftershave and protein powder farts, Captain Dixon stood at the podium to address the shift and announce the tournament would be named for Eric Menser this year. There came that arousal—what was it? sympathy? She threw her hand in the air.

"How do we sign up?" she asked. She'd never raised her hand in muster before.

"It's open to anyone with a glove and the day off," he said and someone in the back of the muster room groaned. The groan didn't bother her; it fired her competitive boil, something she hadn't felt in a long time.

In the heart of her senior year, Brenner tossed twenty-six consecutive scoreless innings. It was a Merrimack Valley Conference record. She hadn't ever gone back to check and see if it'd been broken. But she doubted it had. During the streak, Brenner ate the exact same meals each day: her mother's paprika-dusted ham and egg scramble, a sweaty bologna sub (plastic-like yellow cheese removed) from the school cafeteria, and white spaghetti with watery sauce. She was pitching every other day and ended up throwing all but one of her high school team's innings that year. She'd eaten a lot of those meals that season and sometimes missed the diet consistency, but not the food itself. She was in the local paper constantly; the refrigerator at home was covered in black-and-white clippings. They always seemed to use a photo of her grimacing, the ball clenched at her hip, her body torquing in an unappealing manner in her maroon uniform. Her father used to sneak out of work and she'd see his National Grid bucket truck parked beyond the right field foul pole, his arm hanging out the window holding a cigarette. She knew once they got a lead, any lead, he'd be gone next time she turned off the rubber and pretended to fix the mound dirt.

She fishes through her old jerseys in a box in her apartment closet. In search of her glove, she is brought back to the long days of school, then homework, then out in the backyard where her father had erected a pitching screen with PVC piping and a batting net. Her father had taught her the basics: backswing, downswing, rotation, and grip. But he wasn't versed on the intricacies of the mound because he'd never dedicated an embarrassing amount of time on the craft as she had. She learned on her own to stay tall, keep her body stiff, even her head. She'd stay out there until the mosquitoes roused and signaled the practice's end. And then later, there were practices all winter, one on one with Coach Sullivan, at the loud cages on Tanner Street that were wedged between rival junkyards. She would sometimes synchronize her windup with an adjacent pitching machine that was being fed yellow balls by a fat beer league player, and she'd race the machine, wait for a nod from the man on the other side of the net.

Then when the snow began to melt, she met Sullivan at the field and she threw sessions in the thawing parking lot. People on Rogers Street would slow down or sit in traffic and she'd pound Sullivan's mitt in hopes the passengers could hear the pop of leather, maybe recognize her as the star slinger in the newspaper. No one from the House ever mentioned her athletic achievements, though, probably because she'd attended high school fifty miles south of Barker County, and she'd never bragged about them either. But softball had been her entire persona, and though it was consuming—she didn't go to a dance until her prom, or spend nights at the mall, or date until college—she still wouldn't give it back. When she pitched, coming slowly off the mound to retrieve the catcher's throwback, she knew there was no one better than her on the field, that when a batter got in the box they feared her; she could see them with their weight on their heels. Neither her father nor Sullivan knew what that level of dominance felt like, no one she knew did. It was lonely on the mound; everyone watching you, but no one could change how the ball came out of your hand. She remembers thinking it was the type of loneliness pilots must feel. But the loneliness of the mound merely fostered an incredible ascendancy when the final strike on the outside black was signaled by the umpire's baritone cry, enough so the solitary dominance outweighed any moments of aloneness.

She retrieves her glove from the back of the bedroom closet and the first thing she does is stick her hand inside and shove her face into the webbing and take a deep whiff. It smells like dirt and sweat and glove oil, exactly as she remembers.

At the House, they were issued shirts for training that they are required to wear with BDUs. It is a navy-blue shirt with a badge over the heart and B.C.D.O.C. in gold letters across the shoulder blades. She puts this on along with gray sweatpants. In the kitchen, she attempts to replicate her mother's breakfast scramble. It isn't hard; she tears honey ham lunchmeat into a hot pan and cracks a few eggs over the browning bits of meat, scrambles it all with the head of a spatula. The extra-early morning rise and hot breakfast make her think of her childhood home, the roar of a coffee maker basin draining, her father's cigarette smoke, the thrill of game days.

"Don't let Sullivan warm you up too much," he'd say. "No one knows your arm like you do." Sullivan had played softball, modified pitch, in the air force. He was up there in age but he was the only person Brenner had ever met who could throw harder than her, but not as accurately.

Her father implored her not to work at the House; the job was meant for boneheaded retards, sons of cops too dumb to be cops, not a job for college graduates.

And she eats her scramble and wonders if he was right. She's been there two years and works the tiers and every day has started to become the same. She'd had a career setback when she let Tully toy around with her. So naïve. But maybe it wasn't Tully's fault, but hers, that her father was right and she'll waste her life writing D-tickets and doing so much overtime she can't possibly date. She'll find in the end that her need to prove her father wrong won't give her what she thinks she needs.

———————

IT IS COOL and fall and the trees in southern New Hampshire are at peak foliage, enough so the leaf peepers will only have another week before they miss out. She parks her crossover along the tree line, far enough away from the field for her windshield to be safe from foul balls. The gravel lot is filling; she spots Pelham PD in their baby blue shirts, huddled around a cooler already drinking cans of beer. The pink-shirted clerks from District Court sit on the spectator bleachers behind the backstop and Brenner feels sorry for them but also hopes the House will pull them for their first game. Brenner sips her coffee and notices a few guys from the House on the third base line. Hobson is doing lunges down the length of the field. Sanchez tosses a ball in the air with one hand and picks at his crotch with the other, fanning himself with his loose shorts. And then she sees O'Brien and Tully, it is Tully for sure but he looks a bit thicker, in a good way, mingling with the guys in the dugout, shaking hands. Tully approaches the fence with a smile and says something to the clerks and they laugh. Brenner turns up the radio, a Top 40 pop song she doesn't care for. She ties up her hair in a tight ponytail, puts on her shades, grabs her glove, and gets out of the car.

O'Brien shields his eyes from the bright and painful midmorning sun. He's forgotten his hat. Well, he didn't forget anything. The night before, Tully and O'Brien threw more than a few back after successfully doctoring Pierce. O'Brien slept on Tully's sofa, at Tully's insistence. "Dewies aren't cheap, you know," he'd said. O'Brien is slowly piecing back together the night while trying not to focus on the pain in his toes. He's wearing Tully's son Gabe's too-small cleats, is going to attempt to play right field with Gabe's too-small glove. And then he sees a woman wearing the House uniform come through the swinging field gate. It's Brenner, and at the sight of her he spits into the dirt and thinks about his stupidity from the night before, the conversations he and Tully had and how they led down the Brenner path, and also his Keely admission. Instead of warning Tully that Brenner is there, he swipes his phone from the paint-chipped green bench. He opens Facebook for the tenth time this morning: a friend request to Keely Hankerson, which had been accepted. A private message to her as well: *U up?*

"Let's stretch out," Tully says as he sits down on the bench and tightens his cleat laces. He glances at O'Brien's phone. "Oh, yeah. That was some balls on you last night."

"No," O'Brien says. He wants to smash his phone with Pierce but knows that won't solve anything. "How do you delete a sent message? Can you? Can you delete a message?" Brenner enters the dugout and O'Brien keeps at his phone. He holds his finger on the message until it highlights, but it won't go away. Tully messes with his cleats and doesn't offer a greeting to Brenner.

"Hi, boys," she says. There is a ping of a metal bat hitting a ball into the outfield, the Salem team shagging flies. In the air, it smells like fresh-cut grass and the breakfast sausages Leon, the House cook, is grilling behind the dugout. He has on his whole getup, striped shirt and checkered pants, and is sweating heavily over the grill, patting his head with a dish towel. The House is hosting this year and Captain went all out.

"I can't believe I did that," O'Brien says and tosses his phone into the dirt behind the bench. "Holy fuck."

"Are you our ringer?" asks Tully while still inspecting his cleats.

"I can't play a lick," Brenner says and grabs Pierce from its lean on the fence. She grips it and takes a light, half cut. She holds it like she's done it before. She has a Red Sox hat on, her ponytail pulled through the back.

Teams are arriving and gathering in pockets outside the field's fence. Hollister PD huddles around the grill in their neon-yellow jerseys, some sipping cans of beer and rifling down Leon's sausage, egg and biscuit sandwiches. The clerks and POs from District chat loudly behind the backstop, drinking from Styrofoam coffee cups most likely filled with Bloody Marys. Someone tests the loudspeaker with a "hello, hello" on the mic. Brenner moves outside the dugout and takes a hack with Pierce. She studies the barrel, runs her hand along the fattest part where they'd shaved it down. Tully pops off the bench.

"Her name is Pierce," he says and reaches out for the bat.

Brenner hands it over. "It isn't a boat."

Finally, after almost a year of prodding, Tully confessed he hadn't screwed Brenner in the Property Room like the rumor suggested. A rumor, O'Brien thought, Tully had started. She'd cut him off in the heat of it, he said. The way he worked her was systematic. He sweet-talked her, flirted, pulled back, and then acted juvenilely infatuated. But she found out he was married, which came as a surprise because all along he thought she'd known and that was part of his allure. Which he reasoned was the miscalculation that squashed the whole thing. He talked over an Amstel Light that rested on his chest and he was laid out on the garage floor. He spoke to the silver Fasade ceiling. Tully said after she made it clear she wasn't going to play along, Brenner was all he could think about.

Tully said, "I had this premonition. No. That's not it. What's what I'm trying to say?" He tapped the rim of the bottle.

"A change of heart?"

"Yeah, but like spiritual. It came from somewhere else."

"Epiphany."

Tully snapped his fingers and gave thumbs up in the air above him. He continued. "I always feel empty. And Brenner made me feel emptier, but in a way I needed. Do you know the dread that comes with realizing you overshot your life? I mean, not your entire life, just the meat of it." All through the next few months, he could feel her hand on his pecker, his words, could feel her soft muff hair.

"You only felt each other up and she broke you?"

"She broke me *because* we only grabbed at each other." He said he realized he wasn't gaming her. He had become enamored. And at home, Kathy sensed a change; this wasn't like previous affairs; he moped around the house, and one night he'd gotten drunk and left Brenner's photos open on Facebook on the laptop. When questioned in the morning, he told Kathy everything in hopes of sabotaging his current life.

"I just wanted to fucking bomb it," he said. He was beginning to sound too emotional for O'Brien's liking and O'Brien wished he'd left four beers ago. "Parking lot it."

"And what about the kids?"

"Exactly."

O'Brien grabs his glove and a ball and heads out to the first base foul line, which is freshly chalked, the powdered limestone wet with morning dew. Tully lines up near the bag and they exchange easy throws. O'Brien feels his hangover lift as he gets his body moving. Brenner sits in the grass beyond Tully, stretches with her feet pressed together. He knows Tully is anxious seeing her. Tully's throws become harder and O'Brien backs up a few feet. The outfield is peppered with other teams stretching out, jogging across the outfield grass. Two maintenance workers from the House climb the backstop and hang a banner: FALLEN OFFICERS 2014 IN MEMORY OF ERIC MENSER #64. The House's dugout is filling up: Lt. Hobson wears sporty sunglasses, Dixon smokes a cigarette, and Sanchez wraps chaw in a stretched piece of gum.

"I'm good," O'Brien yells and windmills his throwing arm in the cool air to signal he is warmed up.

"I need a few," Brenner says and jogs toward O'Brien's spot. He watches how she receives the ball from Tully. It isn't awkward. She takes it clean in the webbing. Then she holds the ball in the glove at her waist, steps back with her left leg as if starting a pitcher's motion, strides forward with the same leg, brings the ball high above her head, glove pointed at Tully, and swings her hand down through her hip in a perfect circle and uncorks a pea toward him. He shields his face with the glove and turns his chin from the throw, and the ball smacks the outside of the glove and falls to the ground in front of him.

"Sorry!" Brenner says.

Tully picks up the ball. "Take it easy, Clemens." He throws it back to her. This time overhand, Brenner lobs the ball to Tully.

Captain gets on the loudspeaker and, sounding much like he does when clearing head count at the House, tells the teams to clear the field. He announces the first game: the House vs. Nashua PD. O'Brien wonders if Dixon fixed the first match. The tournament isn't only for Menser. In years past, the winner had bragging rights for a full year. Nashua has the most contact of any agency with the House, bringing new admits in on an every-shift basis, and he can picture Dixon waiting in Booking for Nashua officers to come through the sally port so he can rib them about how his boys kicked their asses.

Inside the dugout, Hobson fills out his lineup sheet. O'Brien's feet hurt. He checks his phone but his world hasn't ended yet. He wonders when it will. Hobson recites the lineup.

"Brenner, short field, batting tenth."

"Hit me leadoff, boss," Brenner says from the end of the bench.

"I don't think so," Hobson says.

"Come on," she says, "what's the difference between first and tenth? Besides, you can get my at-bat out of the way."

Dixon rips his cigarette. "Hit her first," he says. "I think Tully shit his jockstrap playing catch with her." The dugout laughs.

"Oh, you assholes saw that?" Tully says. He looks down the bench to Brenner but she either doesn't see him or snubs him.

Nashua takes the field. O'Brien sits on the bench with Pierce between his legs. He is guarding it. He has resolved to not make any more mistakes because of Tully's lead. If he hadn't gone to shave Pierce, hadn't sat through Tully's misery, then he wouldn't have messaged Keely. If Hobson or Dixon, with their size, get up to the plate with Pierce and put a ball through some poor third baseman's head, some squid PO or gray-haired judge, then he'll have to live with that too. And for what? However anyone in that dugout treated Menser, they'll have to live with that.

O'Brien thinks about the shift where he ratted on Menser for losing his cuff key on Max. He could've helped him, but instead let him fall because it meant propelling O'Brien past Menser on the promotion totem pole. Isn't that what he did? O'Brien doesn't know what his intentions were but does know his actions. He sometimes believes not sparing Menser that day might have been the provocation that started Menser's descent. There is no going back. Menser lived only one life. Nothing will change how he chose not to forgive or rage but to leave.

"I'm up," Brenner says. "Come on, they're waiting."

"Give her Pierce," Tully says. "Let's win this thing."

"It's dead," says O'Brien. "No pop left."

"Plenty left," Tully says.

Brenner grabs the barrel but O'Brien holds tight to the handle. He looks up at her from the bench. She isn't giving up. He doesn't want to get into a tug-of-war with her. He relents and gives Brenner the doctored bat. And for no good reason, he's relieved. He's absolved of whatever happens next. He refuses to envision the alternative scenario, so he pictures Keely reading his message with utter disbelief; first she'd double-check the sender, then she'd smile and with a bite of her lip spend hours deciding what to send back. She's smart, so she'd play through all the scenarios and she'd land on one where she could answer back ever so modestly and there'd be a back-and-forth, innocent banter like notes passed in class. They'd have to be careful, just as if passing notes; their correspondence could be confiscated. It'd be fine. Bomb it. When bombs level a village, a town, a city, you can always rebuild.

Brenner approaches the plate. She tucks her shoulder under her chin. The officer pitching must be a high rank because he is old, mid-sixties, with sneakers instead of cleats, and he heaves a high pitch toward the plate. Brenner shifts her weight, swings the majestic blue, white, and red stick at the ball and ropes it straight back where it came from. Off the pitcher's head, with a sound like the tick of a loud clock, the ball bounces high in the air, suspends, and though from the spectators comes a collective "Ooooo," Brenner still breaks for first with her head down. Clumped dirt kicks up behind her strides, and the ball seems to be rising at such a clip that it will never come down.

DON: Bag and baggage. The two best words a man wants to hear in this shithole.

RAY: That's three words. But I get you.

DON: You don't have to do that, Ray. I can strip my own bed.

RAY: Not your bed anymore. I don't mind. Don, I don't mind. They're going to stick some young kid in here. I know it. Probably some spaz from Nashua with a fucking man bun.

DON: Ask the CO. All the shit you do around here. Mop the floors, lunch duty.

RAY: I did lunch once. And you got me written up because I gave you an extra apple. How you forget these things, Don, I have no fucking clue.

DON: You'll be fine. Just fine.

RAY: Yeah, I'll be upstate soon anyways. Spin the bag. At the top of the net. Yeah, like that, spin it. Here, I'll tie it. Don, I'll tie it. They want it tight in Booking or they'll make you do it again. Haven't you ever B and B'd before?

DON: My first stint here, back in ninety-five, I went straight upstate. I didn't even have a chance to get my shit from the cell. They sent it in a box a few weeks later and half my mail and pictures were missing.

RAY: Don't kid anyone. You didn't have any pictures.

DON: Hand me that folder. That one there, under my coffee cup. I'll leave that cup for you. Give it a good scrub. Don't inspect it. It's fine. It's free. Take it.

RAY: I'm going to need to bleach this thing.

DON: The folder. Get over the cup. Throw it out. I don't give a shit.

RAY: Here.

DON: My daughter. No, the one on the left.

RAY: Holy shit, Don. You couldn't give me some time alone with this picture?

DON: Fuck off. Give it here. This is the only one I got left of her. Cocksuckers lost the rest. Her baby pictures. Gone.

RAY: Ask her for some. Your ex must have a bunch.

DON: I'm going to see her. I can ask her.

RAY: Your ex?

DON: She thinks she can hide. I'm going to find her. She doesn't know what she wants. She never did. I'll swoop in and show her what she's missed. I'm done being the old Don. No more drinking. Or hitting. She'll see. My lawyer got me another shot and I'm not losing it.

RAY: That's good, that's good. Your ride's here. You're not going to hug me, are you?

DON: Not unless you want me to.

RAY: I don't want to see you ever again, Don. Not ever.

DON: I'll try. I'll really try.

ACKNOWLEDGMENTS

I've had many fantastic teachers. I'm grateful for Andre Dubus III for seeing something in me, for teaching me to care about my characters, to go deeper. To my mentors who helped shape the book, thank you for your insight: Mitch Wieland, Ben Nugent, and Tony Tulathimutte. To Drew Johnson, who gave me the best writing advice ever: Read.

I am indebted to Daniel Johnson, who read each phase of this work with an unrivaled editorial eye, who talked me off many ledges, lent me books, and reassured me that my work is important. I'll repay you with beer.

To Andrew Martino, who gave me a quiet space to write. Thanks to Paul Marion, who champions all writers from Lowell, Mass.

To all the correctional officers out there. The job isn't glamorous; it is absolutely thankless; what you do every day matters. To my former brothers and sisters, especially the ones who made the job manageable: McBournie, Jordan, Gordon,

Richard, Barbera, Torres, Frender. Stay safe and watch your back.

Thank you to my agent, Alexa Stark, for believing in me, and in this book, and for getting it out into the world. And to Callie Garnett at Bloomsbury USA, for your hard work and your vision. None of this would have happened without either of you.

Thank you to my family. My children, Calvin and May, who keep me on my toes. My mother, Robin, who showed me how to be strong in a world full of losses. My brothers, Mike and Joe, for support. My sister, Erin, for being my academic sibling rival all those years ago. My father, Rick, who read in front of us, who encouraged my art and is a continued inspiration. We miss you.

This book would not have been possible without the support of my wife, Leah. You keep me going. We did it.

A NOTE ON THE AUTHOR

DAVID MOLONEY worked in the Hillsborough County Department of Corrections, New Hampshire, from 2007 to 2011. He received a BA in English and creative writing from the University of Massachusetts Lowell, where he now teaches. He lives north of Boston with his family.

A NOTE ON THE TYPE

Minion is an old-style serif typeface designed by Robert Slimbach for Adobe in 1990. Visually indebted to the French and Venetian Renaissance, Minion has slightly condensed letterforms which allow for more characters to fit per line of text while retaining a light readable quality. The extensive type family which include small capitals, swash characters, ornaments, and non-Latin alphabets makes Minion a versatile design well suited for setting text for print and screen.